"I couldn't marry someone for the sake of money."

"There are worse reasons to marry, I promise you."
The dark resentment in his voice reminded Brianne
of how devastating marrying for love could be. "I
trust you."

Her gaze snapped up to meet his.

"Yes," he answered her wordless question. "It's true.
This marriage would place a tremendous amount of
power in a woman's hands for the next year. It also
gives my wife access to my family, which means
more to me than anything. I can't think of anyone
else I would trust the way I trust you."

She opened her mouth, but snapped it shut again,
not sure what to say. "Everyone loves babies."

"Not even close," he said with unmistakable
bitterness. "But the second reason I trust you is
this." He took her hand again and held it. Firmly.
"There was a spark between us from the moment
we met."

"No—"

"Don't deny it."

* * *

For the Sake of His Heir is part of
Harlequin Desire's #1 bestselling series,
Billionaires and Babies: Powerful men...wrapped
around th...

D1306924

Dear Reader,

I've been looking forward to writing Gabriel McNeill's story. There's just something about a hands-on man who can fix things, a man who can stride into an old home and make it beautiful again. Gabe might have access to his family's wealth, but he's accomplished so much to be proud of on his own. That's not always easy for him to see, however, since his wife abandoned him and their child. Brianne Hanson, his friend and landscape designer, might have a few buried feelings for Gabe, but she won't stand in the shadow of his glamorous ex-wife.

When a family emergency demands she head home, however, Gabe proposes a plan she can't refuse—a marriage of convenience that will help them both. I have loved writing these McNeill men, especially when they hatch marriage schemes sure to take all the romantic illusion out of tying the knot. Because despite all those practical McNeill plans, romance seems to find them anyway. And the love of the right woman has a way of shifting priorities in a hurry!

I hope you enjoy *For the Sake of His Heir*! Be sure to look for all the McNeill Magnates for more romance and to meet the rest of the family.

Happy reading!

Joanne Rock

JOANNE ROCK

FOR THE SAKE OF HIS HEIR

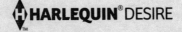

ISBN-13: 978-1-335-97129-6

For the Sake of His Heir

Printed in U.S.A.

Four-time RITA® Award nominee **Joanne Rock** has penned over seventy stories for Harlequin. An optimist by nature and a perpetual seeker of silver linings, Joanne finds romance fits her life outlook perfectly—love is worth fighting for. A former Golden Heart® Award recipient, she has won numerous awards for her stories. Learn more about Joanne's imaginative Muse by visiting her website, joannerock.com, or following @joannerock6 on Twitter.

Books by Joanne Rock

Harlequin Desire

Bayou Billionaires

His Secretary's Surprise Fiancé
Secret Baby Scandal

The McNeill Magnates

The Magnate's Mail-Order Bride
The Magnate's Marriage Merger
His Accidental Heir
Little Secrets: His Pregnant Secretary
Claiming His Secret Heir
For the Sake of His Heir

Visit her Author Profile page at Harlequin.com, or joannerock.com, for more titles.

For my Writerspace family, Cissy Hartley, Celeste Faurie, Susan Simpson and Degan Outridge. Working with you all has been a bright spot in my career. You're awesome all the time, but especially on the days when I'm tearing my hair out and feeling overwhelmed. Thank you for the help, the support and making me feel like I always have a team behind me.

One

Brianne Hanson's crush on her boss had died a swift and brutal death when he'd walked down the aisle with another woman. And she hadn't even dreamed of resurrecting it after his extremely unhappy divorce. She would never want to be that rebound fling a man lived to regret.

But every now and then, the old spark came back to burn her. Like today.

She'd just taken a break from her work in the gardens of Gabe's resort, the Birdsong Hotel, in Martinique. As a landscape designer, Brianne had worked on dozens of island properties before Gabe convinced her to take on the Birdsong as a full-time gig a year ago. It was a job she loved since she had carte blanche to design whatever she wanted on Gabe's considerable budget. He was committed to the project and shared her basic aesthetic vision, so they got along just fine. All business, boundaries in place.

Today, however, was different. She'd stopped by his workshop in a converted shed to ask him about his plans for upgrading the entrance to one of the bungalows. The resort grounds were a never-ending labor of love for Gabe, a talented woodworker who spent his free time handcrafting ceiling panels and restoring custom cabinets.

And damn if she wasn't caught by the pull of that old crush as she stood on the threshold of the workshop. The dust extractor hummed in the background, cleaning the air of particles kicked up by the table saw he'd just been using. Gabe was currently laboring over a curved piece of wood clamped down to another table, running a hand planer over the surface. This segment of wood—a molding destined for a curved archway in the lobby, she knew—was at least five feet long. Gabe shaved the length of it with the shallow blade, drawing the scraper toward him again and again while wood bits went flying.

Intent on his work, Brianne's six-foot-plus boss stared down at the mahogany piece through his safety goggles, giving her time to enjoy the view of male muscle in motion. He was handsome enough any day of the week, as his dark hair and ocean-blue eyes were traits he shared with his equally attractive older brothers. The McNeill men had caused plenty of female heads to turn throughout Martinique and beyond, since their wealth and business interests extended to New York and Silicon Valley. But Gabe was unique among his brothers for his down-to-earth, easygoing ways, and his affinity for manual labor.

With the door to his workshop open, a sea breeze swirled through the sawdust-scented air. Gabe's white T-shirt clung to his upper back, highlighting bands of muscle that ran along his shoulder blades. His forearms were lightly coated with a sheen of sweat and wood dust, which shouldn't have been sexy, or so she told herself. But the strength there was testament to the physical labor he did every day. His jeans rode low on narrow hips, thanks in part to the weight of a tool belt.

And just like that, her temperature went from garden-variety warm to scorching. So much for kicking the crush.

"Hey, Brianne." He turned a sudden, easy smile her way as he put aside the blade, leaving the plank tilted in the brace he'd made to support it. "What can I do for you?"

He shoved the safety glasses up into his dark hair, revealing those azure-blue eyes. Then he leaned over to the abandoned table saw and switched off the dust extractor. As he strode closer, she sternly reminded herself ogling time was over. She needed to keep her paychecks coming now that the last of her dysfunctional family had deserted her grandmother back in Brooklyn. Brianne owed everything—her work ethic, her life in Martinique, her very sanity—to the woman who'd given her a chance at a better life away from the painful dramas at home. As her grandmother became more frail, Brianne hoped to relocate Nana to the Caribbean to care for her.

Besides, complicating matters more? Gabe Mc-Neill had become her closest friend.

"Hey." Forcing a smile to mask any leftover traces of feminine yearning, Brianne tried to remember why she'd come to the workshop in the first place. "Sorry to interrupt. I thought you might be ready to break for lunch and I wanted to see if you had a minute to walk me through your plans for bunga-low two."

He unfastened his tool belt and hung it on a hook near the workbench.

"You mean the Butterfly Bungalow?" he teased, winking at her and nudging her shoulder with his as he walked past.

She'd been resistant to using the names Gabe's new promotions company had assigned to all the suites and villas on the property since they made the hotel sound more like a touristy amusement park.

"Right. Butterfly Boudoir. Whatever." She had to hurry to catch up with him as he headed there now, his long-legged stride carrying him far even though he wasn't moving fast.

Gabe never moved fast.

It was one of the qualities that made him an excel-lent woodworker. He had a deliberate way of doing things, slow and thoughtful, because he gave each task his undivided attention. Tourists who stayed at the resort chalked it up to Gabe being on "island time." But Brianne knew him better than that. He was actually very dialed in. Intense. He just put a charming face on it.

"Let's stop at the main house." Gabe shifted direction on the planked walkways that connected disparate parts of the property and provided the framework for her garden designs. "I've got a drawing you can take with you to see what I have in mind for the bungalow."

He passed two empty cabins in need of upgrades as he approached the back door of the Birdsong Hotel's central building, which housed ten units with terraces overlooking the Atlantic. The dark-tiled mansard roof with dormers was a nod to the historic French architecture of the island. The rest of the building was white clapboard with heavy gray shutters and louvers over the windows—the shutters were decorative unless a hurricane came, and then they could be employed for safety measures. The louvers, another historic feature of many of the houses in downtown Fort-de-France, the island's capital, could be used for extra shade.

"I don't want to plant anything in the front garden that will be in the way of the redesign." Brianne knew better than to think that an upgrade for Gabe only meant a couple of new windows or a better door. She loved seeing the way the buildings took shape with him guiding the redesign, the thoughtful details he included that made each building unique. Special.

She liked to think they made a great team. Her

gardens were like the decorative frames for his work, drawing attention to the best features.

"This project is going to be more streamlined." He brushed away some of the dust on his shirt, then pulled open the screen door on a private entrance in back that led to his office and downstairs suite. "I was planning on talking to you today about some changes in my plans. I'm going to hand off some of the remodel to a contractor."

He held the screen door open for her, waiting for her to step inside. She could see his eleven-month-old son, Jason, seated in a high chair. The boy's caregiver, Ms. Camille, bustled around the small kitchen reserved for Gabe's use. The expansive one-bedroom unit was larger than most. Gabe kept a villa of his own at the farthest edge of the resort and only needed this space for a centrally located office and day care, so it provided plenty of space.

"A contractor?" She must have misunderstood. "You've been personally handling every detail of this remodel for two years because it's your hotel and you're the best on the island. I don't understand."

"Come in." He gently propelled her forward, one hand on the middle of her back while he waved a greeting to the caregiver with the other. "Ms. Camille, I've got Jason if you want some lunch."

The older woman nodded. "Be *en garde*, Monsieur Gabriel," she said, her native French thick in her accent as she passed Gabe a stack of mail. "Our sweet Jason is in a mischievous mood."

Brianne's gaze went to the dark-haired boy

strapped in his high chair, his bare toes curling and butt bouncing at the sight of his father. Two little teeth gleamed in an otherwise gummy grin. Dressed in striped blue shorts and a bright blue T-shirt, the boy banged a fat spoon against his tray.

"I'm on it," Gabe assured her, bending to kiss the baby's forehead, a gesture that clutched at Brianne's heart, making her wonder how Jason's mother could ever abandon him—the child or the father, for that matter.

Theresa Bauder had lived among them for all of six months. She was a beautiful, gifted songstress Gabe met when she'd given up on her dreams to Martinique after a frustrating three years of trying to make it in the music business. Brianne had been envious of everything about the woman, from her eye-popping beauty and natural elegance, to her clear, sweet singing voice on nights when she performed with her acoustic guitar out on the beach.

The fact that Theresa had also landed—in Brianne's opinion—the most eligible of the McNeill men was also enviable. But then, when the woman was expecting Jason, she'd gotten a call from her former manager back in Nashville. A top country artist wanted to perform one of Theresa's songs. Even more exciting, the artist was in talks to do a movie about her life, and wanted Theresa to come out to Los Angeles to play a younger version of her in the film. Theresa left. Her home, her husband, her marriage. To hear the local gossips, Gabe had only gone to LA with her to wait for his son to be born since

Theresa had also decided she didn't want to be a mother with a career heating up. Gabe had said little about it, but he'd returned to Martinique with his son when Jason was just four weeks old.

Brianne took a turn kissing the boy's head, too, as she'd become good buddies with the little one over the last ten months. "How are you today, cutie?" she asked him, her heart melting when Jason gave her a drooly grin. She spotted one of his toys on the counter—a fat green dinosaur—and perched it on the edge of his lunch tray, hopping it closer to him.

"There's something for you, Brianne." Gabe plucked a small envelope off the stack of letters Camille had handed him before setting the rest of the resort's mail in a wooden tray near the door. "Looks like it's from home."

"Thanks." She saw the return address in Nana's familiar handwriting and hoped everything was okay with her grandmother. Distracted, she forgot about her dinosaur game with Jason until the boy poked at the toy.

Dutifully, she made the figure hop around his lunch tray while she considered the letter from her grandmother.

"And sorry to spring it on you like this that I'm leaving." Gabe reached into the kitchen's stainless-steel refrigerator and withdrew two bottles of water, passing one to her. "That's why I'm handing off some of the projects to a local contractor. I need to finish up a few more of the bungalows to accommodate the increase in visitors, but I'm taking Jason to New York and I'm not sure when we'll return."

"You're leaving?" She squeezed the water bottle without opening it, the cold condensation chilling her palms while a wave of disappointment washed over her.

Old crush on Gabe aside, she liked him. Considered him her best friend. He'd given her an amazing opportunity when he'd hired her to design the gardens at the Birdsong, a long-term project that gave her stability and allowed her to be creative. It was a far better job than the temporary gigs she'd been hired for prior to this. She'd met him while helping another landscaper revamp the historic gardens at McNeill Meadows plantation home. Gabe had been building an arbor for his family's expansive compound in Le François. He'd been planning his wedding back then, so she'd ignored the attraction and concentrated on impressing him professionally.

"Yes. I'm going to New York to spend some time with my grandfather." Gabe rifled through a kitchen drawer and pulled out a small sheet of paper, then he ambled over to the round table in the breakfast nook with a view of the ocean. "Have a seat, Brianne."

He pulled out a curved wicker chair for her near the open French doors that led to a side patio shaded by a tall acacia tree. The temperature in Martinique didn't vary much, but on a February day like this, it was less humid and there was a breeze off the water. Brianne never tired of the beautiful weather here after the cold, desperate winters of her child-hood in Brooklyn.

"Your grandfather. You mean Malcolm McNeill?" She'd followed news about his wealthy family online, from the disappearance of his sister-in-law, heiress Caroline Degraff, to the revelation that he had a con-nection to McNeill Resorts' wealthy owner, Malcolm McNeill. Gabe's mother had been Liam McNeill's mistress. Liam had fathered three children by her but then abandoned them when Gabe was just eleven years old. Liam had been married to someone else at that time, and had three legitimate sons based in Manhattan.

"That's right." Gabe drew Jason's high chair closer to the table, earning more gummy grins from his son and another round of spoon banging. "I have a good life here and I'm happiest working on the Birdsong, but I keep thinking it's not fair to limit Jason's future to this place when he's an heir to the McNeill legacy."

The thought of her world without Gabe in it un-settled her. She liked working with him. For him. She didn't want to think about how empty the Birdsong would be without him. And Jason. Her gaze went to the boy, as she thought about all the impromptu lunches they'd had together.

"Are you moving there permanently?" She tried not to let the unexpected swell of emotions show in her voice.

Gabe gave his son a sectioned tray with some sliced-up toast pieces and carrots. Withdrawing the toy dinosaur so as not to distract the baby from his lunch, Brianne clutched it tighter.

"No." He swung into the chair next to her, keeping Jason between them. "Just until I can learn more about the McNeill holdings and convince my grandfather that the terms of his will are prehistoric."

"What do you mean?"

"He's stipulated that all his heirs need to be married for at least a year in order to inherit their share of the fortune." He set down the sheet of paper he'd retrieved from the kitchen drawer; she could see it was a sketch of the bungalow that she'd inquired about earlier, a project that couldn't be further from her mind now. "I don't know if the guy is going senile or what, but my personal experience makes me an excellent case study for why marriage is a bad idea."

His expression darkened, the way it always did when he referred to his ex-wife. It upset Brianne to think Theresa had skewed Gabe's view of love forever.

"You wouldn't be eligible to inherit because you weren't married long enough." She couldn't envision Gabe living in Manhattan or moving in that high-powered business world, but that was probably naive of her. He was a major owner of Transparent, the new social-media software-integration giant run by his brother Damon that seemed to be in the news daily.

"Right." Gabe took a long swig from his water bottle. "I'll never marry again, but does that mean Jason shouldn't inherit? It's not fair to an innocent kid. So I'm going to visit the family in New York and convince Gramps to tweak the will to ensure his great grandson has a fair share of the legacy." He ruffled his son's dark wispy baby curls. "Who could resist this little guy?"

Jason kicked the tray with his bare toes, sending carrots jumping on his plate. The movement preoccupied him, and the baby became fixated with studying the bright orange bits.

"You have a point." Smiling, Brianne reached over to give the baby's feet a fond squeeze, her heart warming at the sight of the two McNeills, one so adorable and the other so…off-limits.

Damn it.

No matter how appealing Gabe might be, he wasn't in any position to start a relationship in the wake of his unhappy marriage. Brianne knew it was too soon to get involved with a man nursing a broken heart. And now? She might never have the chance to be more than a friend.

"So Jason and I are going to spend some time in Manhattan. A few months at least." He tipped back in his chair and reached behind him to drag the baby's sippy cup off the granite kitchen counter. "I've been making drawings of the next few units for you so you can see the changes I'm going to ask the contractor to implement." As he passed her the sketch, his hand stalled on the envelope from Nana. "Should you read this?" he asked, handing it to her a second time. "Your grandmother doesn't write you very often."

As her gaze returned to the shaky scrawl on the

outside of the note, a pang of worry pierced through the knot of unhappy emotions she felt over Gabe's departure. How disloyal of her it was to put her life in Martinique—her complicated feelings for Gabe—in front of her own family.

"You're right." Brianne slid a finger under the envelope flap and raked it open. "I know she doesn't write as much lately because her arthritis has gotten worse."

"All the more reason it might be important if she took the time and effort to write to you now," Gabe added, standing up to grab a damp dishrag from the sink.

He used the cloth to clean up some stray carrots on the tray while Brianne read the brief letter. The scrawl was shaky. Nana took a couple of paragraphs to talk about the failed effort to get a rooftop communal garden in her building, something she'd been excited about. Brianne scanned the rest quickly, thinking she'd take her time to read more closely later. The last paragraph jumped out at her.

I had a little run-in with a mugger yesterday—your standard local junkie, nothing personal. I'm fine. Just a bit sore. It's not a problem really, but makes getting to the market harder. If the offer is still open to have some groceries delivered, your Nana might just take you up on it. I've got plenty to get me through this week, though, so don't you worry.
Love you, child.

"Oh, my God." Brianne's heart was in total free fall.

Her grandmother, the most important person in her whole world, was hurt and alone this week while Brianne had been planting beautiful flowers, living in a Caribbean paradise and mooning over an impossible man. The knowledge sliced right through her.

"What's wrong?" Gabe was by her side instantly, a hand on her shoulder.

"I need to go home." Shakily, she tried to stand, her knees feeling unsteady. "Now."

"Whoa. Wait." Gabe half caught Brianne in his arms, something that at any other time would have brought with it a forbidden pleasure he'd enjoy even though he didn't deserve to.

Today, however, she was clearly distressed. Pale and shaking. What the hell was in that letter?

"I need to go home, Gabe. She's hurt." The broken sound of Brianne's voice stunned him.

He'd seen this woman heft twenty-five-pound bags of dirt under one slender arm and collar snakes with lightning-fast reflexes so she could "relocate" them. He would have never imagined her in tears, but her dark brown eyes were unnaturally bright with them.

"Who's hurt? Your grandmother?" Reluctantly, he pulled his hand from her back, where his fingers briefly tangled in her thick, dark ponytail. He made sure she was steady before he let go of her. Her black T-shirt with an American rock-band logo was wrinkled, the fabric hitching up on one side away from the lightweight cargo pants that were her everyday work uniform.

Her breath came in fast pants as one tear rolled down her cheek. Her normally olive skin had gone as white as the envelope she still clutched. Just a moment ago, she'd been teasing smiles from his son, her beauty naturally captivating even when she wasn't making silly faces to entertain the boy.

"Read it." She thrust the note at Gabe and his eyes scanned the short message from Rose Hanson while Brianne fumbled in the leg pocket of her cargo pants and pulled out her cell phone. "I've been saving money to move her down here with me. I was going to talk to her this weekend when we're supposed to have a video call. I should have been connecting with her every day, but I'm calling her now."

Brianne held the phone to her ear. Gabe could hear someone speaking on the other end, but the call must have gone straight to voice mail message because Brianne punched a button and tried again.

"It's okay." He moved around the high chair so he could be closer to her, and yes, put his arm around her again. He gave her a gentle, one-armed hug, hoping to comfort her somehow as he steeled himself for the shock of pleasure that touching her created. "We'll send someone to check on her. A home health nurse."

Brianne left a message for her grandmother, asking her to call her back right away. Shoving her phone back in her pants pocket, she slumped over the table.

He regretted that he didn't know more about Brianne's family background. All he knew was that her upbringing had been rough enough to make her grandmother cash in the last of her savings to send her off to Martinique with a friend who was retiring to the island. Brianne had been just twelve years old at the time. Her guardian had been little more than a stranger, but she helped Brianne finish her schooling and find an apprenticeship with a local botanist.

Gabe had been caught up in his own drama for so damn long he'd never really gotten to know Brianne as well as he would have liked to. Of course, there was always a hint—just a hint—of a spark with her. He'd ignored it easily enough when he'd been with Theresa, telling himself that the feelings for Brianne were of the creative-professional variety, that he admired her design skills and commitment to her projects.

But there was more to it than that, and it roared to life when he tucked her head under his chin. The scent of her hair was as vibrantly floral as the gardens she tended every day. He couldn't ignore the feel of her against him, the lush feminine curves at odds with her utilitarian work clothes.

"There's no one." She shook her head, her soft, dark hair brushing his jaw. "My stepmother was living with Nana Rose, but then Wendy got a new boyfriend and moved out last month. I've been so worried—"

"I'll find a home health-care service and make a call right now." He pulled his phone from the back pocket of his jeans, hoping Jason's caregiver returned from lunch soon so Gabe could give Brianne his undivided attention.

The protective instinct was too strong to ignore. Brianne had been a positive force in his life during his worst days. And her daily, sunny presence in his son's world soothed a small portion of Gabe's guilt and resentment over not being able to provide a mother for his own child.

"No." Brianne straightened suddenly, tensing as she withdrew from his touch. "It's my job, not yours, Gabe. But thank you." She took out her phone again and keyed in a code with trembling fingers. "That's a good idea to have someone check on her until I can get there."

"Gah!" his son shouted behind him and Gabe turned to see the boy tossing a carrot in the air.

Even though she was upset and distracted, Brianne managed a shaky smile for Jason. She was so different from the baby's mother, who seemed content to leave the parenting to Gabe no matter how often he'd offered to fly to the States so she could see their son. She had no plans to see her baby until Valentine's Day, when she'd arranged a photo shoot in New York with a country-music magazine. As if a child was a prop to show off when needed.

Nevertheless, Gabe would be there to facilitate in the small window of time available for his son to see his mother.

"Maybe you won't have to travel all the way to New York once you have a report on how she's doing from an outside source." Gabe hated to see Brianne return to a life that made her unhappy. No matter how much she loved her grandmother, he knew Brianne had bad memories of the home she'd left behind. "You can have a health-care aide for her as often as you want until you're ready to move her down here."

He wanted to fix this. To keep her happy and comfortable in a life she seemed to thrive in. Something about the gardens and Brianne was forever connected in his mind. She had a healthy vibrancy that was reflected in her work and he knew somehow the hotel wouldn't be the same—nothing would be the same here—if she left.

"I'm taking the next available flight." Her fingers stilled on the phone as she scrolled through screens, her dark eyes meeting his. "That is, I hope you understand I'll need some emergency time away from work."

"Of course, that's a given." He didn't want her to worry about her job. Although selfishly, he hoped her family wouldn't somehow convince her to relocate to New York. He wanted her to return to Martinique eventually since this was his permanent home. He hadn't realized how much he looked forward to working with her every day until he considered the proposition of not seeing her cutting fresh blooms for the lobby desk each morning. "Your position here is secure."

"Thank you." She nodded, long bangs catching on the thick fringe of her eyelashes. "I need to pack in case I can catch something on stand-by tonight." Backing toward the door, she shoved the letter in her pocket. Her cargo pants momentarily pulled tight across her hips.

What was the matter with him that he noticed all the wrong things on a day she needed his friendship? She'd been a rock in his world. He wouldn't allow her to deal with this family emergency on her own when she was clearly upset.

"Don't fly stand-by." He wanted to help her. She never asked for anything and worked hard every day to make the hotel a more beautiful place. She'd been a source of laughter and escape during the hellish weeks after his separation from Theresa.

And he couldn't let her go this way.

"Gabe, I have to." The passion—the vehemence— in her voice surprised him; he'd never heard her use that tone. "She's *hurt*. Someone hurt her. She's eighty years old and she gave me everything I have."

Just like that, he knew he wasn't going to let her go alone. Not when it was this important to her and she was so upset.

"And you shouldn't figure all of this out on your own when you're so distracted and worried." He didn't want her driving when she was still shaking. Or hiring a car from the airport that would take her the long way to Brooklyn because she was too rattled to notice. "I was planning to go to New York anyhow." It made far more sense for them to go together. "I'll take you there myself on my family's jet. Tonight."

"You can't do that." She lifted her arms in the air, exasperated. A long section of dark hair escaped the ponytail to tease against her cheek and she blew it aside impatiently. "You have a son to think about. You can't disrupt Jason's schedule to fly at the last minute."

Brianne gave the boy a tender look, her expression visibly softening as she stroked the back of her knuckle along the baby's arm.

Through the window Gabe spotted Camille, Jason's caregiver, walking up the planked path. He was glad she was back so he could focus on convincing Brianne to travel with him.

"My grandfather has been trying to entice my brothers and me to spend time in Manhattan for months," he explained, pulling Jason out of his high chair and giving the boy a kiss on his head. "I can move up my departure date. My half brother Cam gave me the number of a local pilot who can have a flight plan filed with an hour's notice. If you want to go to New York tonight, I'll call him to take us. It will be faster than navigating the airport crush."

As Camille entered, he passed her the boy and asked her to pack the child's clothes for a two-week trip. He planned to stay longer than that, but would buy more things once they were settled. Camille cooed at Jason and gave Gabe a nod to indicate she'd heard him while he ushered Brianne out of the kitchen and into the afternoon sun outside.

"Gabe, I could never begin to repay you—"

"Why would you have to?" he interrupted, unwilling to let her think in those terms. "I told you, I need to be in New York anyhow so it makes sense for us to travel together. I owe you more than I've paid you, Brianne, if it comes right down to it. But you never hear me complain when you work long hours and contribute more to this place than anyone else. Now it's your turn to accept something extra from me."

She seemed to weigh this, her lips pursing as she visibly wrestled with the idea of arguing. But in the end, she put up both her hands in surrender.

"You know what? For Nana Rose, I'm just going to say thank you and go pack."

"Good." He nodded, already making a mental to-do list, starting with booking the plane and contacting the nanny who would be making the trip with them. "I'll let you know when I've got our flight time confirmed. After we land, we can share a car from the airport, so count on me to bring you straight to your grandmother's doorstep."

"Fine." Her jaw tightened. "That is, thank you."

As she retreated, he wanted to offer more. To suggest additional ways he could help out since she might be facing more medical bills and travel arrangements where her grandmother was concerned. But he didn't want to push his luck with his proud and prickly landscape designer. He had a whole plane ride to talk to her and convince her to let him give her a hand moving her beloved relative back to Martinique. He and Brianne made such a good team at work. Why couldn't they carry that into their personal lives, especially when they were both going through some tough transitions?

The idea held a whole lot of appeal. Maybe that should have troubled him given that he'd just emerged from a disastrous marriage and divorce. Instead, he felt an undeniable pull of awareness that had been absent from his life ever since his wife was two months pregnant and had announced she was leaving him.

Two

Brianne paced outside her cabin in front of the huge strangler fig that listed to one side after years of leaning with the prevailing winds. Suitcase haphazardly packed and ready to go on her tiny wooden porch, she forced herself to take a deep breath while she waited for Gabe to pick her up. Dusk was just settling over the island, casting the resort in shades of pink and peach. Her cabin was already dark from the shadows cast by the wide branches of the tree.

Kneeling down, she scraped a few leaves off the plaque she'd placed there last fall, a final gift bequeathed to her from Nana's friend Carol, who had brought Brianne to this place fourteen years ago as a smart-mouthed preteen. Carol had run out of her retirement funds by the end, her final years in a nursing home having depleted her account. But she'd left the plaque for Brianne, a wrought-iron piece with a Chinese proverb in raised letters reading, "When the root is deep, there is no reason to fear the wind."

Brianne had understood the message—that she needed to rely on the roots Carol had helped her to set down in Martinique, and the values that Nana had tried to impart before Brianne's world imploded with family drama. It didn't matter that Brianne's mom had been a junkie who deserted the family when her dealer moved to Miami, leaving eight-year-old Brianne with a father who was allergic to work but not women. Even then, Brianne had felt like the adult in the house, forging her father's signature on papers from school, instinctively guessing her troubles would multiply if anyone found out how often she went unsupervised.

At the time, she couldn't have known how much worse off she'd be once her dad's girlfriend moved in with them, bringing kids from previous relationships and a surprise half sibling, whose combined support cost far more than the toxic couple could afford. If not for free school lunches, Brianne didn't know how she would have survived those lonely years, where no one remembered to feed her let alone buy her new shoes or check her homework. But when puberty hit, delivering feminine assets no eleven-year-old should have to contend with, she suddenly had all the wrong kinds of attention.

She shuddered at the memories, grateful to hear Gabe's SUV tires crunch the gravel on the far side of the cabin. He'd texted her two hours ago that they could leave at 7:00 p.m., and now here he was—as promised—fifteen minutes before their scheduled departure. Because apparently on a private jet they could take off almost as soon as they buckled into the seats.

Somehow, that kind of favor seemed far more generous than the extra hours she occasionally put in at the Birdsong carefully training a vine over an arbor or watering a temperamental new planting. But for Nana's sake, she sure wasn't going to argue with Gabe about a lift to New York on such short notice. With her bank account, she'd be hard-pressed to afford the rest of the trip and relocating her grandmother, let alone a plane ticket. Still, although she understood the McNeill family could easily afford this kind of travel, she was touched that he wanted to bring her. That was a dangerous feeling to have about her boss, who already appealed to her on far too many levels.

Wheeling her battered duffel bag around to the driveway behind the cabin, she got there in time to see Gabe open the liftgate on the back of the dark gray Mercedes SUV. In a nod to traveling with her employer, she'd dressed in her best dark jeans and a flowy, floral blouse in bright tangerine and yellow that slid off her shoulders and made her feel pretty. Gabe, on the other hand, looked ready to escort an A-list actress to an Oscars after-party, his jacket and slim-fitting navy pants the sort of clothes that came from a tailor and not the department-store racks.

Even his shirt, open at the neck, was beautiful—it was snowy white and embroidered with extra white stitching around the placket. The dark tasseled loafers were, she supposed, his effort to keep things less formal.

"Any news about your grandmother?" he asked.

"She hasn't picked up any of my calls or returned my messages." Brianne didn't know if the phone was dead or the ringer was shut off, but each time she tried Nana's number and got no answer only made her worry more.

"Did you get someone to go over to see her?"

"No." Guilt nipped at her, and she wondered if Gabe could have managed the feat if she'd allowed him to take the task as he'd wanted. "The agency I called said it was too late in the afternoon to schedule a same-day visit. They suggested I call the police if I was worried about her safety."

"Did you?" His blue eyes skimmed over her, making her too aware of his nearness.

Nodding, she tried not to notice how good he smelled. "I did. I wanted to find out if Nana had reported the mugging, first of all, but there's nothing on file with the police. Then, when I asked about someone checking on her, they promised they would send a car out in the morning."

"We'll be there sooner than that," he assured her. "Is this all your luggage?" He reached for the soft-sided bag and retracted the handle into the bottom before he set it in the trunk of the SUV, muscles flexing in a way that pulled the fabric of his jacket taut across his shoulders.

"That's it." She peered into the vehicle and saw Ms. Camille's daughter, Nadine, sitting beside Jason's car seat and called out a greeting before returning her attention to Gabe. "I'm not even sure what I packed. I think I just grabbed something out of each drawer and tossed it in there."

She kept picturing the nightmarish scene of a mugger stealing from her grandmother. She hated that anyone would target someone elderly and frail.

Gabe frowned as he walked with her to the passenger side of the vehicle and opened the door for her. "You should stay with me when we get to New York. My half brother Ian invited me to use his place for the next month while he and his wife are abroad. They have a spacious five-bedroom apartment in a hotel in midtown. There's concierge service, so if you've forgotten anything—"

"No, thank you." She buckled her seat belt and leaned into the soft leather chair, hoping he would drop it. She didn't want to be rude, but she couldn't accept more gifts from him. Her pride wouldn't allow it. She'd been a charity case once and knew how demoralizing it felt to need a handout. "You're already doing enough for me."

Turning to Nadine and Jason, she gave the baby's chubby knee a pat to say hello. Jason tipped his head sideways against the car seat, as if he couldn't keep it upright any longer, but smiled at her sweetly. "Gah!"

The boy was so adorable, his dark curls and blue

eyes already like his father's. She wondered if it made it easier or more difficult for Gabe that Jason didn't favor his mother more. How could Theresa have signed away her rights to raise this precious child?

Gabe took his place behind the wheel and they began the drive inland, leaving the hotel and everything she'd worked hard for in her life.

"Do you know I haven't been on a plane since I arrived here fourteen years ago?" She made the observation as a peace offering, hoping he'd forget about her refusal to take up residence with him in a fancy Manhattan hotel.

It was tough enough to be around him as an employee today. She wouldn't push her luck by getting closer to him personally.

"Are you a nervous flyer?" he asked, steering around a tourist caravan pulled off to one side of the road to snap photos.

She was only nervous about sitting too close to him. His kindness and attention were quickly wearing away the boundaries she'd put up, defenses she thought were solid.

"I don't think so." She didn't recall much about the long-ago journey. She'd cried most of the way, convinced her life was over. "It was a stressful trip, but only because I was being uprooted. I should have returned home long before this."

She had plenty of reasons, none of them good enough to fully explain her complicated feelings about her family.

"I'm glad you're going with me." He glanced her way as he rolled to a stop at a quiet intersection.

The remark was a garden-variety, friendly thing to say. But ever since he'd held her earlier—even though it had been strictly for comfort—she'd been hyperaware of Gabe McNeill. Her throat went dry.

"That's kind of you to say, but I can't imagine it was easy wrapping up your business at the hotel in just a few hours." She smiled over her shoulder at Nadine, needing a distraction from the warmth in Gabe's blue eyes. "Nadine, you must have been surprised to get a call with so little notice."

"I have been asking my mother daily when Monsieur McNeill would be ready to take this trip. I am anxious to see New York City." She grinned widely, her smile so warm and open, like her mother's. "I started packing two weeks ago when I first learned this might happen."

"You see, Brianne?" Gabe downshifted as he turned into the private airfield, a little-used amenity for the island's most privileged. "The trip was meant to be, and it was just as well you lit a fire to get us underway. I might have spent another week tweaking that archway molding."

Grateful to speak about something besides the family problems waiting for her on the other end of their flight, Brianne seized on the topic with both hands.

"You do beautiful work."

"It's an indulgence. A hobby I invest too much time in." His expression darkened as he parked the

SUV beside an exotic black sports car in the small lot. "Now that I'm a father, I need to spend less time on personal pursuits and more time developing my business to provide for Jason's future."

In the back seat, Nadine unbuckled the baby, prattling to him about the great adventure they were going to have.

Brianne followed him to the back of the SUV to help with the bags. She'd never seen anyone restore historic woodwork with as much precision and commitment to craft as Gabe. "What you do is a gift few people have. It's a dying art."

She pulled out her bag and started to reach for a smaller suitcase when a uniformed attendant greeted them, a cart at the ready to wheel their luggage to the plane. A warm breeze blew strands of her ponytail around her neck to stick briefly on her lip balm. She peeled her hair aside, tossing it back behind her shoulder.

"And it's dying for a reason," Gabe replied as they followed the airfield staffer to a gleaming white Cessna with the stairs lowered and ready. "Not enough people care about those kinds of details when you can purchase a prefabricated piece for a fraction of the cost."

He greeted the pilot while the ground attendant loaded their bags for them, leaving Brianne to consider his words. She would have never guessed he'd be so dismissive of the craft he'd spent years honing.

While the attendant ushered them on board the private plane, Brianne weighed what he'd said.

Maybe she didn't know him nearly as well as she thought she did. As if the sleek jet at his disposal didn't already highlight that they came from different worlds, now she questioned how much value he placed on her chosen career field if he viewed his own as simply a "hobby."

Bristling, she told herself not to let it bother her. She was worried about her grandmother and on edge to begin with. She buckled into the deluxe white leather seat as the attendant who saw them on to the plane briefly reviewed some of the amenities. There was a fully stocked bar, Wi-Fi access throughout the journey, global channels available and a simplified cold menu since there would be no server on board with them.

Gabe thanked her, then settled Nadine and Jason in a private compartment in the back. He returned to take the spot beside Brianne, his arm brushing hers briefly as he fastened his seat belt. The pilot pulled up the stairs and locked the exterior door before closing himself in the cockpit for the flight. Not long after, the engine rumbled as the aircraft taxied forward.

Now that they were settled, Brianne picked up the thread of their conversation. "I still can't believe you'd put woodworking down like that. What about landscape design? Is that a dying art best left to wither?"

"Of course not—" he said.

But she wasn't finished. Some of the agitation of the day came out now, her argument picking up momentum as the plane picked up speed.

"Because you can surely purchase a random tree or bush at your local nursery and throw it in the ground. Who needs beauty and refinement when there's a buck to be made?"

As the plane left the ground and gained altitude, the view from the windows shifted from the scattered lights of buildings to a deeper darkness. The cabin lights dimmed automatically, casting them in deep shadow until Gabe switched on the reading lamp over the vacant seating across from them. Only then could she see the level look in those blue eyes as he studied her.

"You think I'm suggesting it's all about money?" His voice gave nothing away.

"That's how it sounds to me. Like your craftsmanship is less important than learning the art of moneymaking at the elbow of a business titan like Malcolm McNeill." But some of the steam went out of her argument at his cool words, and she wondered if she'd misunderstood him.

He leaned forward in his seat and turned toward her, giving her his full attention.

"I have a son to think about. His future is more important to me than any job, passion or hobby." The intensity in his expression was unmistakable. She used to see it, to some degree, when he worked on a restoration project. But this was different.

Powerful.

"I understand that." Truly, she did. "I admire it tremendously given the careless way other people parent their children." Drawing a breath, she ventured closer to her point. "But what if you teach your son that success can be found in things that make you happy?"

Air blew on her from the vents overhead, giving her a sudden chill. Or maybe it was caused by the look on Gabe's face.

"Do I want to teach Jason that it's okay to walk away from responsibilities to pursue any self-centered shot at happiness just because it's shiny and different?" He smoothed the sleeve of his jacket, his forearm resting on the white leather chair between them. "His mother already turned her back on family for a chance at fame. I'll be damned if I make the same selfish choices, too."

Three

Talk about a conversation fail.

Two hours into the flight to New York, Gabe cursed himself for allowing emotions he normally kept in check to bubble to the surface with Brianne. But her words had reopened a wound he'd been determined to ignore. He refused to let thoughts of his ex-wife ruin his relationships—not with Brianne, and most especially not with his son.

Brianne had slipped past his defenses in other ways, too, stirring to life an attraction he'd had on lockdown since they met. And that had given rise to an outrageous idea. Instead of arguing with her, he needed to use this flight to talk to her about working together to help further one another's interests.

There was still time to reevaluate his strategy,

of course. He could keep the scheme brewing in his head to himself and simply escort her to Brooklyn as they'd agreed. In light of the disconnect they had after boarding the plane, maybe that would be the best solution. Except his plan wasn't just about helping himself. It would offer her a face-saving solution to aid her grandmother. It was a way around Brianne's prickly pride to deliver assistance she would otherwise never accept.

He felt Brianne's fingers brush the sleeve of his jacket—the barest of touches to capture his attention. Turning, he found her curled sideways in her seat, facing him. Shoes off, she had her feet tucked under her in the wide leather armchair. At some point during the flight, she had taken her hair down from its ponytail, and the silky dark waves spilled over the lightweight gray wrap she'd pulled around herself like a blanket. In the lamplight, he could see the spatter of golden freckles over the bridge of her nose.

"I'm sorry." She let her fingers linger on his sleeve for just a moment, lightly rubbing back and forth across his wrist, before the touch fell away. "I have no business telling you what's right or wrong to teach your son. I'm so wound up and worried about Nana, I'm not thinking straight."

He set aside his phone, where he'd been scrolling through messages, including a text from Theresa's personal assistant scheduling an "appointment" to have Jason at the photographer's studio in Nashville for the Valentine's Day photo shoot. As much as he wanted Jason to have time with his mother, a magazine spread wasn't what he had in mind. And he worried about Jason's future if Theresa decided to pop in and out of his life. Their son needed stability.

Shoving the troubling thoughts aside, he turned briefly to check the private compartment behind them. No sounds had come from Nadine or Jason in the last hour. Confirming that Jason was all settled, he turned back to Brianne to give her his undivided attention.

"You have nothing to apologize for." He tipped his head against the seat rest and stared up at the jet's contoured ceiling. "You had no way of knowing my concerns for Jason's future." He debated how much more to say about it. But if he was going to propose his new plan to Brianne, he would need to share more with her about his personal life. "You couldn't have possibly known how much time I spent trying to convince Jason's mother to make room in her career so that she could be there for her family."

The old resentment was still fresh.

Brianne tilted her head to one side. "So you want Jason to have more opportunities because Theresa saw only one for herself, and it cost her her family?"

"I don't want my son to ever feel so locked in to one life choice that he can't compromise for the sake of love. Family. Personal relationships." Gabe had offered Theresa so many possible ways to make a family work while she pursued her dream, but she hadn't seriously considered any of them. Stardom and family didn't mix, apparently. She wanted to be "free" to travel as much as she chose without worrying about returning home to the needs of an infant.

He'd told Theresa he would always be there for her, no matter how far she traveled. But she seemed to check out on their marriage the moment something more interesting came along. He could have dealt with that. What killed him was that she'd checked out on motherhood before even giving birth, spending less than a week with Jason before pleading with Gabe to take him back to Martinique so she could concentrate.

Beside him, Brianne pulled the wrap more tightly around her. "I understand. I just hope you find time one day to do what makes *you* happiest, as well."

"For now, I'm content to focus on Jason. There's nothing more important to me than giving him stability. A sense of family."

He had a lot to make up to the boy after being unable to keep his mother around.

"Tell me more about the McNeills who live in New York." Brianne tilted forward to rest her chin on one knee. "Is your extended family large?"

"Besides my grandfather, Malcolm, I've got three half brothers—Cameron, Quinn and Ian. They all married in the last year."

"Because of the terms of Malcolm's will?" Idly, she spun one of her gold rings around her finger with her thumb. The topaz stone appeared and disappeared as she rotated it. Did he make her nervous?

She didn't normally wear jewelry while working. Taking this trip together gave Gabe a different view of her; this was a softer, more vulnerable side of the woman he'd only known through their work. Or maybe he'd never allowed himself to see this aspect of her, knowing he would be drawn to her even more. There was something compelling about Brianne. And something very, very sexy.

He forced his thoughts back to her question. "I'm not close enough with that branch of the family to know their reasons, but it seems highly coincidental they all happened to find true love within months of discovering they wouldn't inherit the family business if they weren't married for at least a calendar year." Then he considered his own brothers and their new marriages. "But both Damon and Jager are over the moon about their wives, so who knows?"

Brianne bit her lip as she considered what he said. Gabe's gaze lingered on her mouth, on the straight, white teeth pressing into her full lower lip. A bolt of hunger pierced right through him.

"And your dad?" she asked tentatively.

He hissed out a heated breath even as he wondered how she would taste if he took a sip of that lush mouth.

"My biological father is out of the picture." He knew that in no uncertain terms. "Apparently Malcolm put Liam at the helm of the company a few years ago and McNeill Resorts started to falter, which is some of what prompted all the new emphasis on the next generation and inspired the unorthodox terms of the will. Liam never placed any importance on family."

"So Jason will be introduced to his great-grandfather, three new uncles, plus their wives." Brianne ticked them off on her fingers, putting the size of the family into perspective. "Are there any cousins in the mix yet?"

Gabe noticed the rose-colored stone on her pinkie ring was facing the wrong way and couldn't resist reaching over to rotate it a quarter turn, letting his fingers brush hers for a second longer than necessary. He wanted to touch her more.

And often.

The awareness between them wasn't going away. If anything, it increased every hour they spent together.

"Cameron's wife, Maresa, had a daughter coming into their marriage. And you heard that Damon and Caroline now have a son, Lucas?" He looked at her for confirmation. Damon lived in Silicon Valley these days, but he'd made an appearance at the family compound in Martinique a few weeks ago. Caroline hadn't even known she was pregnant when she was kidnapped a year ago, so Damon had been shocked to discover they had a son when she returned from her captivity after a bout of amnesia. "Plus Jager and Delia are expecting their first child this summer."

"Jason will be surrounded by cousins." Smiling, Brianne reached up to adjust the vent near her seat. The cool air wafted a soft hint of her fragrance his way, a single fragrant note. "No wonder you'd like closer ties to the family."

She understood. Family was important to her, and

now she recognized how deeply significant it was for him. The knowledge eased the last of his worries about his plan even as the traces of her scent heightened the urge to get closer.

"I want to strengthen that bond." He knew Brianne would appreciate directness. But he'd definitely never envisioned himself making this kind of appeal. "That's why I'm second-guessing myself about my approach with Malcolm." Sensing the time was drawing near to make his pitch, he retrieved the carafe from the small table in front of them. "More water?"

"Sure." She lifted her cut crystal glass and held it out to him. "What do you mean? I thought you were going to try and convince him to remove the marriage stipulation from his will?"

Gabe's hand touched hers briefly as she passed him the glass. He couldn't deny that touching her more often was a definite benefit of his plan. Brianne fascinated him, from her down-to-earth beauty to her easy way around his son. She had values he shared. And yes, she was a sensual, appealing woman.

Just thinking about her made him remember the need to top off his own glass. A cool drink would be a wise idea right about now.

"It occurs to me I'm the odd man out when all of my brothers and half brothers have already fallen in line with Malcolm's wishes." But Gabe knew even that could change, since there was a whole other branch of the family that Malcolm had only revealed to them a few weeks ago. Liam's older brother, Donovan, had disavowed his father long ago, and refused to acknowledge McNeill Resorts or any of the McNeill legacy. No doubt Donovan had started over again in Wyoming, making his own fortune, and no doubt there were potential heirs out there whom Malcolm would try to draw back into the fold. But considering the way Donovan had shunned the rest of the family, Gabe wasn't sure any of those cousins would be interested.

"I thought that was one of your biggest reasons for going to New York?" Brianne's dark eyebrows furrowed as she accepted the glass from him, the gray cashmere wrap sliding off her shoulder when she moved.

"No. My main focus is learning more about their business and strengthening ties with the McNeills for Jason's sake."

"Because you can't allow Jason to be left out of the will. It's not fair that he can't inherit because Theresa chose to walk away." She sipped her water, the ice cubes clinking against the glass. "No one could have foreseen that."

He couldn't help but smile. "Thank you for being defensive on my son's behalf."

"He is your son," she said simply. "He deserves all the privileges that come with the McNeill name."

"I couldn't agree more. But there may be a better way to secure those rights. One that won't put me at odds with my grandfather as soon as I set foot in New York." He set aside the water pitcher and his untouched glass. The jet would be initiating descent soon and he wanted to secure an answer from Brianne before they reached their destination.

"How?" She set her drink aside, too, curious. Unsuspecting.

"I could do what the rest of my brothers have done." He watched her carefully. "I could marry."

Her eyes went wide, jaw dropping. "Seriously?" Then she shook her head, as if none of what he'd said made any sense. "I thought you said you would never marry again?"

That had been before he acknowledged the danger of Theresa deciding she wanted to revisit the custody terms they'd already settled upon legally. Yes, she'd been glad to give him full custody at the time of their divorce. Grateful, even. But if she suddenly decided it would be a marketing hook for her career to have a baby in tow, might she try to convince a judge to overturn the agreement? As much as Gabe wanted Jason to know his birth mother, he wouldn't allow it to happen at the expense of a stable home. Being married could give Gabe an extra edge legally.

Not that he would complicate matters with Brianne by dragging all that up.

"This marriage would be very different," he said instead. "A practical arrangement to serve a particular need." He meant that. But damn. As soon as he'd spoken the words, his brain conjured very different practical needs that might be served if he wed in name only.

And had Brianne in his bed.

"A marriage of convenience?" The words came

out on a horrified half whisper almost drowned out by the drone of the plane's engines.

He'd managed to scandalize her. Not quite what he was going for. So he concentrated on laying out the terms the same way he'd sketch out a plan for a building, helping her to see the final product before she dressed it up with landscaping.

"A legal union for twelve months and a day. Just long enough to ensure Jason can inherit his share of the McNeill legacy." He studied her, surprised she hadn't made the connection yet about where this was headed. About her role in it. But he knew she felt the spark of attraction that he did, even if she ignored it as studiously as he had.

He needed to get past that careful facade now. Acknowledge the heat for what it was—a sensual connection that could make the next twelve months incredibly rewarding for both of them. Reaching across the leather armrest between them, Gabe took her hands in his. Her skin was cool to the touch. The pale pink paint on her short nails shone under the dome light.

"Brianne." He slid his thumbs over the insides of her palms, stroking light circles there before he met her dark gaze again. "I want you to marry me."

Breathless, Brianne felt mesmerized by the man and the moment. The proposal was so ludicrous, so impossible, it was like one of those delicious dreams where she knew she was dreaming but didn't want to wake up. Because in a dream, a woman could explore forbidden things like a sexy attraction to her wealthy, gorgeous boss. In that moment between waking and sleeping, there was no harm in feeling that tingle of hot awareness down both thighs. Along the lower spine.

In her breasts.

The simple stroke of Gabe's hands had that same effect on her. But unfortunately, Brianne was not dreaming. She needed to wake up and put a stop to all this right now before things ventured into even more forbidden territory.

She needed her job, now more than ever. Too much to risk a misstep with Gabe, no matter how much she wanted to run her lips along his whisker-rough jaw and inhale the woodsy cedar scent of him.

"Very funny." She tugged her hands out from between his, tucking them between her knees. That way, she wouldn't be tempted to touch him back. "I can see where marrying your gardener would be a nice, in-your-face gesture to your megarich grand-father, but I'm sure you'll come up with something better than that."

"I'm not joking." Gabe's voice was even, his expression grave. "My back's against a wall with Malcolm's will, and a marriage is the simplest way to ensure my son's future."

In that moment, she realized he hadn't been joking. Which made the proposition all the more unsettling.

"So marry. Fine. I get it." She knew how much value he placed on giving his son every advantage in life. She admired that about him, but she couldn't possibly help him. "But you have to know I can't take part in a scheme like that. There's far too much for me to lose."

His gaze narrowed slightly. "You haven't let me outline the full extent of the plan or what you stand to gain." He seemed to shift gears, appealing to her on a business level. "Half the reason I want to do this would be for your benefit. If you help me with the marriage, I will extend to you every advantage that comes from being a McNeill in return. That means no more worrying about your grandmother or where she'll live. As my wife, you'll have access to the best doctors and round-the-clock nurse aides, if you need help caring for her."

The possibilities spun in front of her eyes, as she contemplated the way Gabe could wave the wand of his wealth and power over her life and fix things— just like that. It brought into sharp focus what he was offering.

Not just to her. To Nana.

"I couldn't marry someone for the sake of money." What kind of person did that make her? She shook her head. "It's too...bloodless. Not that I have any great romantic plans for my future, but I also never pictured myself heading to the altar for the sake of a hospital bill."

Shifting positions, she straightened in her seat and placed her feet back on the floor. No more cozy intimacies with this man. It was too risky. Too tempting.

"There are worse reasons to marry, I promise

you." The dark resentment in his voice reminded Brianne of how devastating marrying for love could be. "And the reason I thought of you, Brianne, is not just because this marriage would benefit you. But also because I trust you."

Her gaze snapped up to meet his.

"Yes," he said, answering her wordless question. "It's true. This marriage would place a tremendous amount of power in a woman's hands for the next year. It also gives my wife access to my family, which means more to me than anything. I can't think of anyone else I would trust the way I trust you."

"Why?" She shook her head, not understanding. "We only just work together. I mean, we share a few laughs and things, but—"

"Two reasons. One, you're good with Jason. I see how gentle you are with him. How your eyes smile when you look at him. You can't fake that kind of warmth or enjoyment of kids."

She opened her mouth, but snapped it shut again; she wasn't sure what to say. "Everyone loves babies."

"That's not true. Not even close," he said with unmistakable bitterness. "But the second reason I trust you is this." He took her hand again and held it. Firmly. "There was a spark between us from the moment we met."

"No."

"Don't deny it. We both ignored it and that was good. That was the right thing to do." He squeezed her fingers gently and that warmth trickled through her veins again, like an injection of adrenaline. "Not many women would have ignored that spark. At the risk of being immodest, Brianne, the McNeill wealth attracts way too much feminine attention, and I haven't always done a good job of appreciating the women who wanted me for my own sake versus the ones who wanted to get close to the lifestyle our world affords."

She'd never thought about that before, but knowing what she did of human nature, she wasn't surprised, either. Had Theresa been one of those women? She didn't dare to ask; she was too overwhelmed by this shocking outpouring from Gabe.

"You, on the other hand—" he tipped up her chin to see into her eyes, and the warmth of his touch there made her mouth go dry "—you respected my marriage and my family, right through the day it all went up in flames and long afterward. That's how I know I can trust you."

"Gabe." She couldn't find the right words, was still stunned by his admission. He'd known about the attraction all along and hadn't said a word. Hadn't acted on it. "If what you're saying is true, that there is a...spark—"

"Do you doubt it?" He loomed closer.

Her heart beat faster.

"Just, let's say that there is an attraction." The word scraped her throat. "It would be playing with fire to get married and play house. I can't throw away my job—my future—for the sake of one year. I wouldn't be able to work for you anymore."

The fact that she'd tossed out an excuse rather

than outright saying "hell, no" made her realize she was actually considering it in some corner of her mind. She guessed that he sensed as much since he leaned forward, a glint in his eyes that she recognized from when she'd seen him close a deal. He spotted an advantage.

"We'll have a prenuptial agreement. You can name your terms for a settlement so you don't need to concern yourself with work."

"I like my job." It was more than just a paycheck. She lived at the Birdsong. The gardens were a work in progress she hoped to develop for years to come. "I had plans to make the grounds an attraction people would visit there just to see."

"So we'll add in job security as part of the settlement." He shrugged like it was such a small concern.

The plane dipped on a patch of turbulence and her belly pitched along with it. Gabe's arm went around her shoulders automatically, steadying her.

She didn't even realize that she'd grabbed him— his thigh, to be exact—until the plane was sailing smoothly again. Releasing him, she peered up into his eyes and tried to regain her equilibrium.

The heat glittering in his gaze didn't come close to helping.

"We'd have to keep ignoring it." The words slipped from her lips before she had time to think them over, making her realize she was already mulling over how this crazy idea might work.

"What?" He tensed, his arm tightening a fraction around her shoulders where he still held on to her.

"The attraction." She plowed forward, knowing she might regret it but unable to turn down the offer of help for Nana. The level of help that Gabe could give her—the comfort his wealth could provide for her—was the kind of thing her selfless grandmother deserved in her late years. There was nothing Brianne wouldn't do to repay Nana Rose. "We would have to keep a lock on any attraction, the same way we've always done." That was nonnegotiable. "I don't want to feel like I sold my soul for the sake of Nana's care."

His eyes dipped to her lips. Lingered for a moment, then came back to hers. "I would respect your wishes, of course."

Did he know how much his heated glance sent her pulse racing?

"And I would need to trust you. You'd have to promise not to use that attraction to…" She'd never been a woman who minced words, but this was new territory. "What I mean is, you can't try persuading me to go outside my comfort zone, even if you see I might be caving. *Especially* if you see I might be caving."

Instantly, he removed his arm from around her shoulders.

Already, she mourned the loss.

"Done." He nodded. All business.

And shouldn't that be a lesson to her? Gabe McNeill was well versed in sensuality. If he could shut it down that fast, no doubt he could apply it when necessary, as well. She needed to be wary around him.

"Then, if you're really serious about going through with this—"

"I can have our agreement drawn up by noon. We can apply for a marriage license tomorrow before the offices close for the day. Assuming you retained your U.S. citizenship?"

He was serious all right. She nodded.

"So did I. And New York only requires a twenty-four hour waiting period after we apply, so that makes it simple."

So for Nana's sake, she would find a way to make it work.

Before she could second-guess herself, she blurted, "In that case, you havè yourself a deal."

And with one look at his heat-filled eyes, Brianne had the feeling she was in over her head even before she said "I do."

Four

She'd said yes.

An hour later, Gabe had to remind himself of the fact as he peered over at Brianne beside him in the limousine. Her expression was tense. She didn't look like a woman who had any reason to celebrate as the lights from the bridge flashed on her face while they crossed the East River and headed into Brooklyn. The drive from the airport had been quick thanks to light traffic, and Gabe had sent Nadine and Jason ahead to the apartment in midtown Manhattan in a separate vehicle so the baby could have some rest after the long trip.

Which left Gabe and Brianne alone for this next leg of the journey. Their first trip as an engaged couple.

The drive into Brooklyn's Bushwick neighborhood was a far cry from how he'd celebrated his first wedding proposal. He'd taken Theresa to Paris to propose over dinner—a romantic night he'd wanted for a woman who adored being romanced. In the long run, what had it meant to her? While he regretted that he hadn't even given Brianne a ring with his proposal, he still felt relieved that this marriage agreement was nothing like the first one. They both knew what they were getting into. There would be a prenuptial agreement. Clear terms for the future. He'd messaged his attorney's office from the plane after Brianne agreed to his plan and she'd seemed content to let him make the arrangements.

No one needed to be disappointed. On the contrary, they could both enjoy the peace of mind that came with knowing their interests were well protected. That they were helping one another.

So why did Brianne's dark expression make her look like she'd just made a deal with the devil?

"Are you okay?" he asked, laying a hand on her arm hidden inside the cashmere wrap she'd worn in place of a jacket.

The clothes were plenty warm for Martinique in February. Not so much for New York. He'd have to see about having a winter wardrobe delivered for her. He wished he could put her at ease, but maybe she was just keyed up about her grandmother. No doubt she was worried.

"I didn't realize how strange it would feel to come home." She stared out the limousine window into a dark and silent park as they sped deeper into Brooklyn. "I was so sure I didn't miss this place, and yet now..." She shook her head. "I have so many memories here. Not all of them bad, though."

"You've never really said why your grandmother sent you away." He hoped maybe talking would help her relax. Or at least distract her from worrying about her grandmother. He'd called a private health-care service to meet them at the Brooklyn address in case Brianne needed help moving her grandmother. She hadn't protested when he made the call now that they'd agreed to the marriage deal.

For his part, Gabe was glad to focus on helping her. Maybe that would alleviate the twinge of guilt over how he hadn't mentioned that a marriage might help him with custody if Theresa decided to revisit the terms they'd agreed to previously.

"My family life was complicated even before my father remarried." She turned to stare at an all-night diner lit up in bright pink lights. "Then, once he brought Wendy home, I was the odd one out."

Something her father should have never allowed to happen. Gabe wouldn't let anyone near his son who didn't care about the boy. Jason had already been abandoned by his mother.

"You two didn't get along?" Gabe asked, trying to envision her life as a kid.

Brianne had told him once that her mother had a long-term problem with prescription painkillers and had run off with her dealer when Brianne was only eight, leaving her in the care of a disinterested father. Even then, the grandmother had been Brianne's role model, the woman who kept her family together.

"Something like that." She glanced up at the high, neon vacancy sign flashing on a nearby hotel. "My stepmother had a jealous streak. She didn't see me as a threat when I was nine, and gladly ignored me. But once I hit puberty, she turned vicious if anyone noticed me."

Defensiveness for the girl she'd been had him straightening in his seat. He was angry on her behalf.

"Vicious how?" he asked, keeping his voice even. "Did she hit you?"

"No. Not quite." She pivoted her shoulders toward him, dragging her attention from the window. "Some shoving once or twice. Mostly, she raged at me to keep my, um, breasts to myself while trying to wrench my too-small clothes around me to cover more." She shook her head, dragging weary fingers through her thick waves. "A real class act."

And Brianne had been just a kid. Damn.

His hand found her wrist, and he squeezed gently.

"No wonder your grandmother wanted you out of there." He hated to think about an adult manhandling her like that when she was a child. "I'm so sorry you went through that."

"I've heard Wendy is on medication now for some of her issues." She crossed her legs, her foot swinging with the motion of the limousine as it made a sudden stop for a red light. "She was taking reasonable care of Nana and helping out with the rent up until a couple of months ago."

He sincerely hoped he didn't run into the woman who'd treated Brianne that way.

"Where's your father these days? He doesn't participate in caring for his family?" Gabe would trade almost anything to have his mom back. Losing her to cancer while he was a teen had devastated him far more than when his father quit showing up.

He couldn't imagine a son not stepping up to take care of a mother. Although, now that he thought about it, how would Jason feel about Theresa one day if he ever discovered how easily she'd walked away from them both? Resentment simmered.

"One of his sons with Wendy has had some success as a singer on YouTube, believe it or not." She lifted an eyebrow, showing some skepticism. "My dad followed their oldest, Tyler, to Los Angeles to help 'manage' him."

"You have some half siblings, too, then," he observed as the limo rolled to a stop in front of a string of old brownstones on Bushwick Avenue.

"A few." She nodded distractedly, her attention focused on the brownstone. "Tyler was born while my mother was still in the picture, so he's only a few years younger than me. This is it." She pointed to the building with no lights on, sandwiched between two others that were still lit and humming with activity—a loud television blaring from the first floor of one, a couple kissing feverishly on the front step of the other.

The five brownstones looked just alike—same wrought-iron fire escapes, same sets of garbage cans at even intervals. A bright Laundromat sat on the corner of the block, machines still spinning and door open to the street even though it was almost midnight.

He wanted to ask her more, find out why none of the half siblings were checking on their grandmother, but Brianne was already launching herself toward the limo door. Gabe opened it for her before the driver had gotten around the car. He didn't blame her for the hurry.

"Do you have a key?" He helped her from the vehicle, sliding an arm around her waist as she stepped onto the curb under a blinking fluorescent streetlamp.

"I do—unless the locks have been changed." She held up a cloth change purse embroidered with roses. "Nana gave me this as a going-away present." She opened the metal fastening and showed him the interior lined with pink satin. Inside, there were two keys and a coin. "A quarter so I could always call home and keys for the doors."

Her voice wobbled with emotion.

Noticing the limo was drawing attention, Gabe reached to take the keys, then guided her up the stairs of the brownstone. The kissing couple had quit breathing down each other's throats to stare. Normal curiosity, maybe. But he'd feel better when he got Brianne safely inside.

"Good." He worked the bigger key in the outdoor lock, feeling the mechanism give way. "The home health-care workers should be here any minute. I told our driver to circle the block until we text him so there's room for the transport vehicle."

"I hope we don't need it." He could sense the tension tightening her shoulders and he didn't even try to resist the urge to rub away the knots as they stepped into the darkened hallway. A night-light from a floor above shined dully on the warped staircase.

Brianne turned to the left, her feet gravitating toward what must be her grandmother's first-floor apartment. A withered clump of evergreen boughs tied with a red ribbon still hung on the door—a holiday leftover too long neglected.

"She's going to be in good hands," Gabe assured her, checking his phone when he felt it vibrate, his hand falling away from her shoulder. "That'll be the health-care workers now."

Headlights flashed on the road outside, where a bigger vehicle double-parked while Brianne knocked on the apartment door.

Waited.

Rang the bell.

He glanced over at her, trying to gauge what she was feeling. How he could help. He remembered those brief awful months of his mother's illness and how it had devastated him. Sure, he'd been a kid. But he knew even now dealing with that—seeing a loved one deteriorate in front of your eyes—would level him.

"Okay." Brianne drew in a deep breath. "I just need a minute with her first. Just to see her with my own eyes."

"I'd like to go in with you." He didn't trust the rest of her family from the little bit he'd learned about them. What if the stepmother was helping herself to the apartment while the grandmother recovered? Or someone else?

Just because no one answered the door didn't mean no one else was inside. A surge of protectiveness had him itching to tuck her under his arm again.

"That's fine." She nodded, withdrawing the second key from her purse. "Just not anyone else. Not yet."

"Of course." He planned to make this reunion as easy as possible for Brianne. That had been his part of the wedding bargain—the main reason she'd agreed to his terms. "I'll tell them to wait until you're ready."

Nodding, she turned the key in the door of apartment 1A and stepped inside.

"Nana?" Brianne's legs were shaking even more than her voice. She cleared her throat and tried again. "Nana, it's me. Brianne."

She didn't want to frighten her grandmother, but then again, she wanted to lay eyes on her fast. What if she was more hurt than her letter had suggested? Heading toward the apartment's only bedroom, she felt for a light switch on the wall near the tiny stove in the galley kitchen. A weak bulb over the table buzzed to life in the cold apartment. It couldn't be more than sixty degrees. The kitchen was clean enough, though. No smells of spoiled food. One clean cup and plate sat in the sink drainer.

With her hand on the bedroom doorknob, she leaped back at a sudden, rough voice shouting on the other side.

"I've got a gun this time, you son of a—"

Gabe was between Brianne and the door instantly, shoving her behind him.

"Nana?" Brianne's heart beat triple-time. She recognized that scary voice meant to put the fear of God into misbehaving children. "It's Brianne," she blurted, relief making her legs weak. She clutched Gabe without thought, gripping his upper arm and taking strength from his shoulder as she tipped her head to it for just a moment. "I flew home when I got your letter."

The bedroom door swung wide.

Gabe scuttled sideways with Brianne, still keeping himself between her and her grandmother. Around his shoulder, Brianne could see Rose Hanson, dressed in a pink floral nightgown and matching housecoat, her matted gray braid threaded with a bedraggled ribbon.

"Do you have a weapon, ma'am?" Gabe asked, even as Brianne stepped out from behind him and rushed toward Nana Rose.

"Just this." She held up an old smartphone that had seen better days, the case cracked away on one side. "My son showed me an app that sounds like an automatic rifle, but I'll be damned if I could find it." Her hazel eyes turned toward Brianne then, her expression softening as she lifted a stiff hand to skim over Brianne's cheek. "You scared the pants off me, girlie."

"I was so worried you were hurt and I didn't know how to reach you." She closed her eyes and two tears leaked free as she hugged her grandmother carefully. She didn't think anyone would notice she was crying in the dim shadows from the lamp over the kitchen table. "Are you okay?" Leaning back, she tried to see Nana's face while surreptitiously scrubbing away the tears. "It's so cold in here."

"Who's he?" Nana asked, stepping more fully into the kitchen. She was favoring her right side. She looked the same, but smaller, as if time had eroded away a few inches from her height and the plumpness that used to animate her features. A Latina beauty— her mother's family had come to New York from Puerto Rico—Rose Hanson had miles of thick, wavy hair, deep golden skin and an expressive smile. Her hair had gone fully steel-gray, but it was as long as ever judging by the braid. "You never told me you had a beau."

"This is Gabriel McNeill, Nana." Brianne's eyes went briefly to Gabe's. He still stood close to her grandmother, looking ready to steady her at a moment's notice. "I told you about him. He owns the Birdsong, where I work."

Nana eyeballed him thoroughly, the same way she'd done to any friends Brianne had brought over to her house to play after school. Brianne had lived with her father two blocks away in a building that she'd heard had been ripped down years ago.

"You're a long way from home, Gabriel McNeill," Nana observed, swaying slightly on her feet as if a wave of tiredness had just hit her. She looked pale, but Brianne couldn't tell if that was just simply because she'd aged, or if she had hidden injuries and wasn't feeling well.

"We're newly engaged, Mrs. Hanson," Gabe announced, reaching to pull out a chair from the kitchen table for her. "I wanted to be with Brianne for this trip." He gestured to the seat. "We're worried about you."

Nana eyed the chair warily. "No need to cosset the old lady." Her chin lifted. "I'm fine. I just wanted a little help getting some groceries until I get better."

Something in the older woman's expression made Brianne doubt she was telling the truth. Stubborn and proud, Rose Hanson had been a performer in her youth, a torch singer at a New York jazz club with a backup band of her own. There were posters of her around the apartment—or there had been long ago—advertising performance dates. Now the walls looked barren in the living area. The whole apartment looked like someone had come in and stolen most of her things.

Had she pawned extra furnishings for cash?

"Get better how?" Brianne gave Gabe a private nod, hoping he'd understand she was ready for the home health-care workers to come inside. "Where are you hurt?"

"Nowhere." Rose shook her head while Gabe moved quietly toward the front door, his phone already in hand. "I don't need the cavalry, honey, just some bread and eggs." She ambled awkwardly over to a cupboard near the sink and tugged it open. "I'm down to some cracker crumbs."

Brianne glanced in the cabinet to find nothing but some cracker packs pilfered from a restaurant—the kind they give you with an order of soup.

"Ow." With a wince of pain, her grandmother lowered her right arm slowly, then cradled it.

Brianne ached for her. She wished she could have arrived sooner.

"You're not fine." Brianne could hear Gabe admitting the health-care aides out in the hallway of the building. "Nana, we brought a nurse to check you out. We want you to come with us tonight and stay with me until you're fully recovered."

The older woman's gaze darted to the door, where Gabe was entering with two younger men dressed in dark cargo pants and T-shirts, ID badges around their necks. One carried a medical kit and had a stethoscope around his neck. Armed with friendly smiles, the health-care workers introduced themselves to Nana and were able to help her into the kitchen chair.

One of the guys brought out a small spotlight, flooding the kitchen with a brightness that brought into stark relief how dingy and dilapidated things looked. Another pang of guilt hit Brianne. She should have come to New York sooner.

"I haven't had so many people in my kitchen since

the nineteen-sixties," Nana grumbled at the men before launching into tales of her heyday and the wild after-parties she used to host on Bushwick Avenue following her performances.

"Gabe and I will just be right here," Brianne called to her, backing away to afford her some privacy while they asked questions and checked over her arm.

"How does she look to you?" Gabe asked, one shoulder against the pantry door in the cramped space, a look of concern in his blue eyes.

No matter what else became of this contract marriage in the coming year, Brianne felt intensely grateful to have him there with her. To have the help of professional nursing aides to look after her grandmother.

"Exhausted, wary and hurt," she blurted, unable to hold back her worries from him. "She has no food in the cabinets and most of her possessions are gone. I don't know if she's been pawning things over the years or—"

Rapid-fire pounding on the front door interrupted her.

"Excuse me!" A shrill feminine shout accompanied the knocking. "Open up!"

Brianne froze, recognizing the caustic tone. For a second, she was eleven years old again, scared speechless.

Gabe glanced through the peephole, not seeing her distress. "A five-foot-two tornado with red hair and a considerable amount of cosmetics for one in the morning," he announced before turning around. "Anyone you know?"

"Better open up before she shrieks down the whole house," Nana called from her seat on the chair, her head popping up over the shoulders of the two men who were taking her vitals and assessing her bruises.

"I thought she moved out," Brianne replied woodenly, reminding herself she wasn't a kid anymore. She'd known that coming to New York would mean facing family members, not just her grandmother.

The pounding continued along with the shouting. Expletives peppered the demands to open the door.

"She sure did," her grandmother replied. "And I made her return her keys, too."

"Would you like me to call the police?" Gabe seemed undisturbed by the racket, his attention fully focused on Brianne. "She's causing a disturbance."

Unwilling to appear weak in front of a man who knew a completely different person from the scared kid she used to be, Brianne shook her head.

"I'll have to speak to my stepmother sooner or later. Might as well get it over with now."

Five

Gabe pulled open the door during the next round of pounding. He couldn't help but feel a bit gratified when the obnoxious guest stumbled forward a step at the sudden admittance and tripped on the thin braid rug. He steadied the woman enough to keep her upright, like a gentleman should. And that was going to be the extent of the chivalry he extended to the stepmother responsible for making Brianne's early adolescence a traumatic time.

The wiry woman with hair dyed bright crimson glared up at him as she shook off his hand. She wore a loose men's T-shirt and a shrink-wrapped mini-skirt, her hair sticking out at odd angles like she'd just woken up despite the massive amount of eye makeup. Her narrowed gaze swept the scene, dismissing him and skipping over Rose until she spotted Brianne.

"Look who decided to grace us with her presence." The woman straightened to her full height—which wasn't saying much—and curled her lower lip in a sneer. "Should I be impressed you finally decided to show some loyalty to the family?" Brianne's stepmother marched toward the medics still working on Brianne's grandmother. "Just what the hell is going on here?"

Brianne tracked her progress, but didn't move to intervene. Gabe half expected her to collar the intruder and relocate her out the door the same way she would have done with a reptilian visitor to her garden. But she looked rattled. Gabe made a half step toward her grandmother before Rose spoke up.

"Pipe down, Wendy," Rose told her easily, swatting in her direction like the woman was little more than a pesky fly. "If you cared what was going on in here, you could have shown up last week when I could barely move," Rose chided her. "Heaven forbid that spoiled brat of yours who lives next door come over here personally to check on me. Does she have a deal with you where she only calls when there might be some drama?"

Brianne seemed to find her voice, stepping forward. "Who lives next door, Nana?"

"None of your business," her stepmother retorted, glaring at her as she wavered precariously on her spiky heels. Had she been drinking?

Gabe wanted to get Brianne away from her ASAP. The woman certainly made no secret of her dislike.

"Vanessa lives over there now," Rose answered while the health-care workers wrapped her right arm in a splint. "Wendy's oldest girl. I'll bet she was outside on the stoop canoodling with that big lug she calls her boyfriend when you arrived, Brianne. Scrawny baggage couldn't run to the phone fast enough is my guess."

Gabe liked Nana. He'd been prepared to respect and admire her even before they met, just knowing that she was responsible for sending Brianne to Martinique, for giving her a better life than she'd had in New York. But now, meeting her in person, he couldn't help but smile. He heard some of Brianne's toughness in this woman's voice. Understood now where that came from.

Wendy put her hands on her hips, angling between the health-care aides to fume at Rose. "You should be happy she's keeping an eye on your apartment. She called me because she thought a gangster was after you when she saw a limo pull up." She eased back a step when one of the medics put out a hand to keep her at bay. Wendy looked at Brianne again. "I never guessed Ms. Big Time would pay us a visit, and in a limousine, no less."

"I'm not here to see you," Brianne retorted, arms folded. "I'm taking Nana home with me."

"You're doing what now?" Rose asked, leaning forward to let one of the health-care workers put a coat around her thin shoulders.

It was freezing in the apartment, making Gabe wonder if the lower temperature was for cost savings or if there was a problem with the heater. Either way, it was obvious that an injured elderly woman shouldn't be staying here alone. Brianne had been wise to fly to New York as fast as possible.

"Rose isn't going anywhere," Wendy informed her, chest thrust out like she was about to start a fistfight. "You can't just waltz in here after all this and start making decisions that don't concern you."

Gabe wondered why the woman cared one way or another if she wasn't involved with her mother-in-law's life. Or was it her former mother-in-law? He wasn't even sure Wendy was still married to Brianne's father. It brought Gabe no joy to learn that Brianne's family life had been even more convoluted than his own. At least he'd had the stability of one parent, who'd tried her best to raise him, Jager and Damon the best she could.

One of the health-care workers stood from where he'd been wrapping bandages around Rose's arm. "It appears Miss Rose has a broken ulna bone, and possibly a couple of broken ribs. I'd like to get some X-rays as soon as possible."

Wendy sucked her teeth and made a skeptical sound but the announcement seemed to give Brianne new resolve. She darted past her stepmother to kneel beside Rose's chair.

"Nana, there is a medical van outside," she explained softly. "We can go to the hospital tonight."

Gabe watched them, hoping Brianne would convince her. He knew his future bride wouldn't rest until she'd made sure her grandmother was properly cared for. And because that meant everything to her, it meant a whole lot to him, too. Before he could hear Rose's response, however, Brianne's stepmother sidled in front of him.

"So who are you if you're not a thug?" she asked, eyeing him with open curiosity.

"Brianne's fiancé. Gabe McNeill." He didn't offer his hand.

"McNeill?" The woman's lips pursed tight. "Rose told me you were Brianne's boss."

"Not anymore." He tried to sidestep her, to rejoin Brianne.

But Wendy proved shifty. She stayed right with him, her gaze narrowing. "I don't see a ring on her finger."

"It's being sized." The truth was not her concern, for one thing. And for another, he didn't trust the gleam of interest in her eyes. He wasn't going to allow her to make any hassle for Brianne.

Behind her, the medical workers helped Rose to her feet while Brianne found her some shoes.

Wendy pointed a finger at him. "You're the one who was married to the uppity wife." She nodded, satisfied with herself. "I read about you in one of Brianne's letters."

Brianne glanced up, shooting an apologetic look his way.

"Those letters were to me, you snoop," Rose called over. Her hearing had to be very good to key in on that. "And leave that man alone," she scolded while she slid into a pair of scuffed boots.

Gabe said nothing; he was finished with the conversation. He knew Brianne well enough to know she hadn't spilled intimate details of his life to anyone. There was no positive spin to put on his divorce, after all. Then again, he wondered how much Brianne had shared if she thought her letters were only being read by her grandmother. Could her stepmother know anything about him or his family that could prove awkward down the road?

He wasn't worried for himself. But if Wendy tried to stir trouble for Brianne, or for his son, there would be hell to pay.

Brianne scooped up her grandmother's purse from a chair in the living room before she made her way closer to Gabe.

"I'm going to the hospital with Nana. I need to ride in the van with her."

"Of course." He heard the worry in her voice. "I'm going with you."

"You don't need to do that." She shook her head, her gaze tracking Rose's slow progress across the kitchen as the older woman shuffled along with the help of an arm from one of the health-care workers. "You'll want to be with Jason if he has any trouble adjusting to a new environment."

"Nadine is completely in her element with any child-care crisis, and she has my number if she needs anything at all. Jason is in good hands. I'm going with you."

He wanted to help her. To spend more time with her. And yes, put that ring on her finger as soon as possible. He had enough problems of his own dealing with the aftermath of his divorce and being a good father to Jason. He didn't need a bitter stepmother suspicious about the validity of his upcoming union.

The sooner he married Brianne, the better.

"Shhh. We don't want to wake her." A man's soft voice outside Brianne's door drifted through her dreams the next morning.

Blinking and disoriented, she stared at the moldings on the tall door of the unfamiliar room. Dull winter daylight filtered over her. Her new home for the foreseeable future, she remembered groggily. She'd arrived here at Gabe's half brother's vacant apartment after four in the morning. She'd been just awake enough to help Rose, who now had a cast on her arm, into a bedroom on the second floor before falling into the king-size bed that Gabe had directed her toward on the main level.

"Gah!" A baby shout-squealed just outside of the door to her suite, making her smile. There was a soft scuffling noise and then a trailing echo of "Gah, gah, gah!" as the sound moved farther away.

Clearly, father and son were up and about this morning. Envisioning the two of them playing together kept her smile in place.

Her soon-to-be husband and temporary son.

The smile faded.

What on earth had she agreed to yesterday? Sitting up in the most exquisite sheets she'd ever felt, Brianne shoved her tangled hair behind her shoulder and glanced at the old-fashioned bedside clock, only to discover it was almost noon. Muted views of falling snow were visible through the half-drawn shades, and the sounds of the city on the street below were so different from the birds she normally heard in the morning. Here there was the dull rumble of traffic: brakes and horns punctuated with the occasional shrill whistle or shout. A siren in the distance.

Slowly, reality sank into her foggy brain. She'd agreed to marry her boss in exchange for help with her grandmother. In the clear light of day, without the mesmerizing power of Gabe's seductive blue eyes on her, Brianne realized how much was at stake now. Her pride? Too late to salvage that. Her heart? She'd have to watch it like a hawk to keep herself from getting too swoony over her sexy fiancé.

But those costs were nothing compared to that precious baby boy of Gabe's. Jason had already been semiabandoned by his mother. Gabe had been devastated when Theresa insisted he return to Martinique with the baby while she pursued her career alone. How was it any better for Brianne to form an attachment to the child and then walk away a year later? Jason wasn't going to understand how important the temporary marriage was for his "legacy." What would a toddler care about that?

Throwing aside the covers, she hurried into the shower and rinsed off fast. She towel-dried her hair, brushed her teeth and threw on some wrinkled clothes from her suitcase before padding out into a library full of books about architecture and design. Beautiful prints of the New York skyline covered the walls in the few spots there were no books or windows.

She followed the sounds of baby giggles and found Nadine with Jason in the kitchen. The boy whacked a wooden spoon against a silver mixing bowl on the floor.

"Morning." Nadine offered a cheery smile from her spot at the kitchen counter, where she sat with a map of the city and a highlighter. "I hope we weren't too noisy."

Jason stared up at Brianne from his spot on the marble tiles, his shoulders bobbing as if he had a song in his heart. He shook the spoon at her. She bent to smooth his dark curls and helped him to tap his makeshift drum.

"Goodness no. I should have gotten out of bed ages ago." Straightening, she tried to glance into the next room, down the hall, but couldn't see past a set of partially closed French doors. "Do you know if my grandmother is awake?"

"It's been quiet upstairs. Mr. McNeill said you got home really late." Nadine folded the map, then slid her papers and phone to the far side of the stainless-steel countertop. "A nurse's aide arrived about ten this morning, though, and she's upstairs in the study outside of your grandmother's bedroom in case she needs anything."

"Great." That was a thoughtful gesture from

Gabe, who'd arranged for rotating nursing staff the night before while they'd been waiting for Nana to get her X-rays. "I'll go introduce myself in a minute. Is Gabe here?"

She needed to see him. Speak to him. Explain that they must put Jason first and foremost before they went through with this marriage.

"In the office." Nadine pointed through the French doors. "It's on the right through there."

"Thanks." Brianne wouldn't have thought twice about joining him in his workshop back in Martinique, but this place was a whole different world from the Birdsong Hotel.

Views of Central Park blanketed in frosty white glittered through the windowpanes, with more flurries swirling in the air. She hadn't seen snow since she was a kid and part of her still longed to run outside and play in it. But seeing her grandmother's injuries and living conditions had made her more committed than ever to take more responsibility.

But the snow wasn't the only difference in the scenery. Here, there was no escaping the vast divide between the world she came from and the one Gabe moved in. She remembered the icy chill of a cheap studio apartment in winter like her grandmother's. Gabe McNeill, on the other hand, was no stranger to homes like this one, a full-amenity hotel with a prestigious Fifth Avenue address. He'd introduced her to the wonders of concierge service and twenty-four-hour in-room dining the night before, explaining how she could order food from the hotel's restaurants anytime.

He traveled with a nanny for his son. Produced home health care for her grandmother at the snap of his fingers. Brianne owed him so much. And she was so out of her league with this man.

"Gabe?" She tapped the back of her knuckles on the half-open office door. Brianne peeked inside to see him wave her forward.

Cell phone tucked between his ear and his shoulder, he pointed toward a silver tea cart with a coffee carafe and two small warming trays with domes. It was a breakfast invitation that her grumbling stomach answered before she'd made up her mind to stay. He was already wheeling the tea cart closer to the window, next to a couple of gray wingback chairs.

"I came here to spend time with Malcolm and the rest of the family," Gabe said into the phone, juggling it from one hand to the other. "I hope to spend time with him. So if he's not going to be in New York, maybe I should head out to Wyoming see him." He paused, listening. "Sure. Let me know either way, Ian. And thanks for the apartment."

He disconnected the call while Brianne stood in the middle of the office, watching him. She wouldn't have guessed he'd been up until four in the morning with her and then out of bed before her to play with his son. He was dressed more casually today in a pair of jeans worn in all the right places. The black button-down he wore was another one of those custom-made pieces that fit him perfectly, his nipped-in waist and broad shoulders accentuated just enough to make a woman's pulse leap a bit.

"Morning." He greeted her with a warm smile that made her remember how easy it had been to strike up a friendship with him. "Come join me for breakfast. I ordered the darkest roast coffee in the whole hotel, just the way you like."

She realized she'd been staring. Gawking, really. Apparently having a marriage proposal on the table was counterproductive to keeping her thoughts platonic. But damn it, they'd started as friends. Surely she could still have a reasonable conversation with him.

"Thank you." The fragrant scent had her moving toward the wingbacks. "I didn't mean to interrupt, but I need to talk to you."

"You're not interrupting anything." He waited for her to sit and then pulled the domes off the breakfast trays. "I've been anxious to speak to you, too." He poured her a cup of coffee and passed her the mug. "Did you sleep well?"

"Like a rock, thank you." Memories of waking up to his voice skated over her skin. "I was shocked at how long I was out."

"You needed it after yesterday." He filled a white china plate with eggs and toast, then passed that to her, too. "You must be hungry."

Taking a second dish, he arranged more food on it for himself before sitting in the chair beside her. Brianne fixed her coffee, adding the cream, while she thought about how to raise the issue of their temporary marriage.

"I feel like I dreamed half of what happened yesterday," she admitted, taking a careful sip of her drink.

He stilled for a moment, then set his breakfast on the end table nearby. "If you're referring to the proposal, I hope it was a good dream." He reached for a flat box under the tea cart and set the heavy wooden case on the ottoman in front of her. "Although this might make our arrangement feel more real."

Flicking open the metal clasp on the box, he lifted the lid to reveal an expanse of blue satin filled with diamonds.

Wedding rings glittered and winked in the light. Her breath caught at the dazzling display, millions of dollars' worth of jewels casually there for the taking. Perhaps he heard her small gasp because Gabe rose and came around to stand behind her chair, his hands suddenly on her shoulders. She felt a solid, steadying warmth. More than that, even.

Affection. And yes, desire. Her heartbeat stuttered.

Leaning closer, he kissed her temple and stared into the box with her.

"I'd like you to choose a ring for our wedding, Brianne."

Six

Anticipation firing through him, Gabe angled back to see her reaction.

The tense worry pulling her eyebrows tight wasn't exactly what he'd been going for.

"What's wrong?" Shoving over the display case, he shifted to sit on the ottoman across from her so he could see her better. "You're not having second thoughts, I hope."

Unease dimmed his excitement. He'd already filed for the marriage license. He needed her to go through with this for the sake of his grandfather's will and to bolster his position with regard to custody of his son. But more than that, he wanted Brianne in his life. The attraction they'd been ignoring wasn't going away this time. Spending the last twenty-four hours together had only strengthened their connection, something she must recognize, too.

"Not exactly." She shook her head, the dark, damp strands of her hair swishing against her white sweater. With no makeup and fresh from the shower, she looked the way she did at the start of so many work mornings, except she hadn't tied back her hair.

Natural. Unaffected. Beautiful.

He laid a hand on her knee, a privilege he wouldn't have allowed himself just last week.

"Is it your family? Are you worried about anything?" He had tried to make things as easy as possible for her the night before, but she wouldn't hear of leaving her grandmother at the ER alone and he didn't blame her.

"We agreed to the marriage for our own personal reasons, and they still stand." She set aside her plate. "Already, you're helping me so much with my grandmother, and I couldn't be more grateful. But I woke up this morning thinking about Jason. How's this going to affect him? We're going to get attached to each other…" She blinked fast. Shook her head. "That is, Jason and I—we'll spend a lot of time together this year. And where does that leave him twelve months from now?"

The concern in her voice, the worry in her eyes, should have touched Gabe. He knew that—and somewhere inside, he was moved by her thoughtfulness. Her ability to put Jason first. But more than anything, her words lit a new fire under the old resentment at

Theresa for never voicing any such concern about her own defection.

With an effort, he swallowed back that bitterness in order to reassure Brianne.

"The fact that you care how he'll feel means you're going to handle it the right way." He let his thumb stroke the top of her knee. "Every parenting book I read says that as long as you're caring and trying, you're ahead of the curve. And I know you'll do both those things, Brianne. You care, and you'll try to make any separation easier for Jason."

Her gaze slid from his down to where he touched her, but he couldn't pull away. Not until he knew she understood.

Slowly, she lowered her hand to his and held it, effectively stilling his movement. Or taking comfort from him? He couldn't tell with Brianne. She'd asked him not to press the attraction, but they were still friends. Still capable of offering one another comfort.

"I had a lot of people walk away from me when I was a kid, and I know how much it hurts," she confided, her dark eyes bright with emotion.

"I would never stop you from seeing Jason afterward." He wanted more relationships for his son. "I want love in his life, Brianne."

"Thank you." She blinked away the tears in her eyes, seeming to tighten the reins on her composure. "That helps."

How often did she do that? he wondered. Hold a piece of her heart back for safekeeping?

"And don't forget, not everyone walked away from

you when you were a kid. Yes, your grandmother sent you away," he reminded her gently, "but did you ever doubt her love for a minute?" He didn't need an answer from her since the truth was obvious. "Kids feel it when the grown-ups around them are trying to do the right thing. They sense that care and connection."

She nodded. "I know what you mean." She smiled slightly. "Nana's pretty great, isn't she?"

"Yes. Just like you." He gave her fingers one more squeeze and then let go, turning to pick up the ring box again. "So let's not worry about the future anymore and focus on important things like diamonds and breakfast." He handed her back the white china plate while he slid free the ring closest to her, holding it up to the daylight through the window. "What do you think of this? A round diamond is supposed to be the most stable in a setting. I thought you'd like that since you work with your hands a lot."

"Gabe." She pointed her fork at him between bites. "Those diamonds are all outrageous. You have to know they are too over-the-top for a down-to-earth girl like me."

"Carat size is nonnegotiable." He liked that teasing light in her dark eyes. But he set down the ring with the round diamond. "How about this one? The jeweler told me it's technically called a rose cut, which is an old-fashioned way to polish a diamond, apparently." He held up another ring for her to see the facets. "I thought you might like it as a nod to your grandmother. Another Rose."

He had her attention now. She set down her plate again and leaned closer.

"I've never heard of a rose cut." Taking the platinum set piece from him, she tilted it this way and that.

"I hadn't, either, until this morning, when the jeweler dropped these off." He popped another ring from its satin slot. "This one is a pink diamond that's rose cut. Double the roses."

"It's stunning." She ran one fingertip along the band, her hand brushing his.

She studied the ring and he watched her. He could tell this one was the winner, and liked that she'd chosen something so overtly feminine.

"Would you like to try it on?" He took the first ring from her hand and set it on top of the case, keeping her fingers captive all the while.

"Are we really doing this?" Her breathless voice skipped along his senses like a tentative touch.

"Yes." He rolled the platinum band back and forth between two fingers, the pink diamond glinting. "We absolutely are."

He needed this marriage.

And even more? He wanted this woman.

"Then I guess it can't hurt to try it on." The grin spreading over her face made him smile, too.

Damn, but he wanted to make her happy.

The urge to kiss her was strong. Any other time, with any other woman, he wouldn't have thought twice about giving in to that urge. But Brianne had asked him to hold back.

So he would. At least for a little longer.

Turning his attention to her hand, he lifted her ring finger and slid the pink stone into place. Outside the office, he could hear Jason banging on pots in the kitchen while Nadine tried to sing accompaniment.

"A perfect fit," he announced, admiring the way the jewel looked against her deeper skin tone. "Like it was made for you."

"How did you know what size?" She peered up at him, her dark waves taking shape as her hair dried.

"Last night in the emergency room, I held your hand for a minute and got a feel of that topaz ring you were wearing yesterday." The move hadn't been calculated, but feeling the band around her finger had reminded him he needed to seal their bargain with an engagement ring. "When I let go, I drew what I thought the size was on a piece of paper from the nurses' station. The jeweler matched up the drawing with a real size after I sent it over this morning."

"I guess that shouldn't surprise me. You're always superdexterous when you're working with wood." She flexed her fingers back and forth, as if getting used to the feel of it. Her gaze darted self-consciously toward him for a moment before she lifted a miniature sweet roll from her plate and took a bite, chewing thoughtfully. "You're very good with your hands."

Because he was staring at her, he could see the moment the comment took on a sensual dimension in her thoughts. Her eyes widened. Two fingers covered her lips as if she could still catch the words she'd just uttered.

"I'm glad you've noticed." He imagined applying that skill set to his bride's luscious curves. Envisioned the slow stroke of his hand up her thigh. Over her hip. "I hope you'll consider putting my hands to work for the common good in the months ahead."

"The common good?" Skepticism dripped from her words. "I'll keep that in mind if I need any historic woodwork restored."

"Surely you can be more imaginative than that," he replied, enjoying the way the heat spiked between them. Wanting her to consider the possibilities this marriage offered. "You work in a creative field, after all."

"Wicked man." She straightened in her seat and faced him head-on even though her cheeks were flushed pink. "I'm not sure my job is all that creative, but landscaping definitely has taught me how to wade through…BS."

He had to laugh at that one. "It's not BS if I mean every word." He stood, not wanting to pressure her when he hadn't yet completed the primary objective: marriage. "But how's your schedule look for tomorrow afternoon? I spoke to the same court clerk who married Jager and Delia, and he said he could make a trip out here if we're ready for the wedding ceremony by noon tomorrow."

"Really? So soon?" Blinking, she shoved to her feet and seemed to take a few calming breaths. She tugged her phone from the side pocket of her cargo pants. Pressing the button to light up the screen, she glanced back up at him. "That would make us husband and wife in twenty-four hours."

"Why delay?" He couldn't afford to lose the advantage now that she'd said yes. "I had a few gowns brought in this morning along with some flower options. Would you like to see?" He'd had the household staff hopping from the moment he'd rolled out of bed this morning, but it turned out his half brother employed extremely competent help.

Then again, Ian's personal assistant had seemed glad for the work after managing a quiet apartment for the past week. Which was a good thing, since Gabe wasn't letting anything stand between him and Brianne, or their wedding.

"You're serious." Brianne shook her head. "I don't need to see the gowns now. I'm just surprised how fast everything is coming together.

"As promised." He'd made additional arrangements to leak the news of the wedding so that Theresa would hear.

Not that she would care one way or the other, but Gabe wanted his ex—and her lawyers—to know that Jason was living in a secure, two-parent home. Sooner rather than later.

"I'd hoped my grandmother could be one of our witnesses, but I'm not sure she'll feel up to it." Brianne worried her lower lip.

Fixated on the movement, he wished he could swoop in and capture her mouth with his, saving her lower lip from the torment. But he didn't want to push her more off-kilter when he needed to nail down plans for a wedding.

"We can see how she feels in the morning. But it might be easier to get a couple of staffers to be our witnesses so Rose can rest. The nurse was going to ask her doctor about increasing the pain medications for a couple of days so your grandmother can get some extra sleep and recover." His phone buzzed with an incoming message and he picked it up to check it.

"I'll go upstairs and speak to the nurse right now." Brianne didn't move, though. She put a hand on his arm. "Is everything okay?"

Inwardly cursing the frustrating news he'd just received on the phone, Gabe mentally reworked his plans to accommodate the sudden turn of events. He turned off the screen.

"Just a note from Ian, the half brother I was speaking to when you first came in." He huffed out a breath of irritation as he pocketed the phone. "Apparently my grandfather won't be returning to New York until he can convince his estranged older son to see him."

"Even though you traveled all this way to meet with him?" She tilted her head, the same way she did when she stared at a new landscaping space, as if she couldn't quite take its measure.

He was having a tough time figuring it out himself. But he'd come this far to solidify his son's legacy. He wasn't going to turn around and go home or let Malcolm McNeill off the hook. He planned to meet the man face-to-face. Become an irrefutable part of this family to protect Jason's interests.

"He's an old man in failing health. He wants to conserve his resources and minimize his own time in the air." Gabe only hoped Brianne would be on board with the plan B taking shape in his mind.

He'd simply have to go to Malcolm.

Brianne frowned. "I don't understand. How long will we stay in New York to wait for him?" Her dark eyes searched his.

"We could avoid waiting around if we went to him. Your grandmother has around-the-clock nursing care, and Jason is in excellent hands, so we're not needed here for a few days." He couldn't deny there was a whole lot of appeal to having Brianne all to himself. "What do you say to a honeymoon in Wyoming?"

Twenty-four hours later, Brianne was so nervous that the delphinium petals in her wedding bouquet were jiggling in her hand as she waited beside her grandmother's bed. She'd spoken to the nurse about increasing Nana's dose of pain medication for the next few days so she could heal and sleep. Brianne approved of the plan wholeheartedly, except she sure wished she could get Nana Rose's blessing before she said her vows in Gabe's half brother's living room.

What a crazy few days it had been.

"Nana?" Brianne sank to the edge of the bed. Her grandmother's face was peaceful, her bandaged arm resting on the cream-colored linens.

Was it wishful thinking, or did her color look a little better today? Nana had been so weary by the time they returned from the emergency room, her skin pale and breathing shallow.

"Try again, honey," the gray-haired nurse, Adella, urged from the doorway, her starched white uniform bearing little resemblance to the colorful scrubs the ER staff had sported. "I've been holding off her next dose so she has a chance of hearing you."

"Nana?" Brianne said again, louder, lowering a hand to her grandmother's thin shoulder.

Already, she could hear Nadine calling for her from downstairs. No doubt they were waiting for her to start the wedding ceremony.

"Brianne," Nana replied in a scratchy voice from the bed. "What's wrong?"

Her grandmother hadn't even opened her eyes. Brianne squeezed her hand, careful to touch only the uninjured arm. Behind her, she heard Adella intercede with Nadine to wait another minute before interrupting them.

"Nothing's wrong, Nana. Can you open your eyes?" She really wanted her grandmother to see her in the outrageously beautiful gown made of imported Italian lace and satin. "I'm getting married to Gabe today, and I wanted you to see me. You're the closest family I have."

With a slow flutter of lashes, Nana's eyelids lifted.

"Oh, child. Look at you." Rose's eyes roamed Brianne from head to toe. "Stand up so I can take a peek at that dress."

Brianne couldn't help a twinge of self-consciousness even as she got to her feet. She was romanticizing this when the ceremony was a formality for a marriage that would end one year from now. But what if she never married again? A wistful piece of her heart wanted to savor the joy of twirling in this beautiful lace mini-dress and matching jacket. She'd left her dark hair down to fall over one shoulder. Her pale blue sling-backs echoed the deep indigo of the delphiniums she carried. She had never placed much importance on appearance, often dressing to deflect attention after her stepmother's criticism during her preteen years. But today, she felt beautiful.

Gabe had given her that.

"I'm getting married downstairs." And then she was hopping on a plane again, to share a honeymoon in Wyoming with her outrageously sexy former boss. "The city clerk is already here, Nana, but I wanted you to know."

Nana's smile was fleeting as her eyes closed again. For a moment, Brianne thought she'd fallen back asleep, but then came a whispered rasp from the bed.

"Be true to yourself, Brianne." Nana Rose mumbled the words, her lips barely moving. "You can't make anyone else happy until you're happy."

Brianne's throat burned a little at the advice that didn't quite apply since she and Gabe were marrying for very particular reasons. She wished she wasn't deceiving the person she loved most in the world. But she'd done what she'd come here to do.

Now it was time to get married.

"Thank you, Nana. I love you." She kissed her grandmother's forehead. "I'm going to take a honeymoon for a few days, but I'll be back before you know it, and Adella is going to stay with you."

"Love you, too, Bri. And don't you dare rush home to sit with your granny when you have a hot-looking husband to enjoy." Her eyes opened long enough to give Brianne a sly wink. "Go on and have fun, honey."

"I'll...um. Okay." She didn't have a response to that one when she had no idea what a honeymoon for a contract marriage would be like. Platonic, right? Her heart beat too fast; she was fairly certain she was lying to herself. She might have used up all her restraint where Gabe was concerned while he'd been married to someone else.

Especially now that it was clear she had his full attention. The attraction was undeniable.

"Bri?" Nana stirred again. "Wendy is breaking in to the apartment when I go out. If you want anything out of there, better lock the windows before she takes what little I have left."

A moment's horror made Brianne almost trip. No wonder Nana's apartment had been so bare. Anger burned through her that someone who'd married in to their dysfunctional family could be so cruel. The strains of a violin drifted into the room, the lilting classical composition at odds with the dark implication of Nana's revelation.

"I'll make sure she doesn't take anything else."

Brianne would ask Gabe if they could have the apartment contents cleared and moved to a storage facility until it was time to move her grandmother to Martinique. "Should we ask the police to get involved? I'm sure we can recover—"

"No need." Nana held up a weak hand and waved off the idea. "I hid all the best stuff where she'd never think to look."

"Where?" she pressed, fearful her grandmother would fall back into a drug-induced sleep before revealing her secret hiding place.

Nana's satisfied chuckle assured Brianne she wasn't sleeping yet. "In the broom closet there's a false wall behind the cleaning supplies. Ms. Wendy would never bother to pick up the ammonia, and that's the truth." She pointed an arthritic finger in Brianne's direction. "Go get married, girlie, and have extra fun for your Nana who doesn't have a man in her life right now."

"Okay." Brianne hurried back toward the bed and gave her grandmother's cheek a second kiss. "Feel better soon, Nana."

Backing away, she almost ran in to the nurse, who was hustling closer.

"Don't you worry about a thing, miss," Adella said, drawing up a fresh needle to attach to the port in Nana's arm. "Her vitals are strong and I'm going to take good care of her with the help of two respite workers. She'll be much improved by the time you return."

"Thank you." Brianne wanted to hug the woman for the tender way she nursed Nana. "I'm so grateful."

"Call me anytime you're worried or want an update," Adella urged before gesturing toward the door. "Now don't make that handsome groom of yours wait any longer. Many blessings to you both on your wedding day."

Brianne's chest tightened again at the reminder of all the people she was deceiving, and would continue to deceive all year long.

"Thank you." She tried to smile like any other bride, but the truth was, her delphinium petals were quivering even harder as she walked out of her grandmother's room and headed toward the stairs.

Now she was nervous not just about the wedding, but about her stepmother's underhanded schemes to get her hands on Nana's few belongings. As soon as the ceremony was over, Brianne would solicit Gabe's help to secure that Brooklyn apartment and clear out the contents.

Strains of classical music rose from the living room. A lone violinist played something festive. Not a traditional wedding song, but the sound was rich and beautiful.

Would Gabe have gone to the trouble and expense of a violinist for their justice-of-the-peace vows? Her sling-back heel caught on the last step and she steadied herself on the banister.

Of course he would. Just look at how much he'd spent on the selection of dresses—seven to choose from—and shoes. Then there was the pink rose-cut diamond and matching wedding band he would slide on her finger any moment. He was a good, thoughtful man, and he'd made it very clear he wanted her to be happy.

If only he knew that's what she was afraid of. What if he made her so happy she couldn't walk away?

Reaching the formal living room, Brianne spotted Nadine and Jason playing off to one side while two household staffers—a maid and Ian McNeill's personal assistant—signed a book on the antique secretary. Gabe had hoped one of his half brothers might be able to attend—especially since one of them lived in the same building. But Ian, Quinn and Cameron were all out of town this week, leaving Gabe and Brianne to celebrate the wedding with the few people on staff.

A female violinist wearing a long, velvet skirt sat in a straight-backed chair in the farthest corner of the room, her head bowed over her instrument as she glided over the strings to produce the exquisite Mozart melody filling the room.

The most commanding presence, however, was Gabe himself. His dark jacket and silver-colored tie suited him, lending a formality to their day wedding. The clothes were perfectly pressed, and his hair, still damp from a shower, was sleeker than normal. It made her realize how starkly handsome his features were without any hair falling over his forehead in appealing disarray. Today, he looked every bit the billionaire, from his thin timepiece to his polished loafers.

She was so busy gawking, Brianne almost forgot she was the bride until the whole room grew quiet.

Every head turned to her as she hovered uncertainly at the archway leading into the gray, modern living area. She felt all the eyes upon her in a vague way since the only gaze that really mattered was Gabe's. His blue eyes seemed to speak to her across the room, the slow simmer of appreciative heat giving her courage to lift her chin.

Uphold her end of their hasty bargain.

Almost as soon as she had the thought, the violinist began the recognizable strains of the "Wedding March." It didn't feel like a marriage in name only with that music playing, with the delphiniums wavering in her bouquet, the ivory-colored lace skimming her thighs as she stepped deeper into the room. Her pulse quickened and her gaze locked with Gabe's.

How many times had she sneaked hungry glances at him over the last year? How often had she reminded herself he was off-limits?

Now he was all hers.

For an entire year.

As she drew even with him near the window overlooking Central Park, Brianne handed off her bouquet to Nadine and thought about her grandmother's words.

Make yourself happy first.

It didn't apply. Shouldn't matter since she wasn't marrying Gabe for real. But how could she *not* ima-

gine making herself happy with this sexy and end-
lessly capable man looking at her like he might kiss
her at any moment?

She faced him when the violin music halted and
the city clerk launched into the celebrant's speech.
They hadn't written vows so they were using the
simplest ceremony possible.

Too nervous to hear any of it, Brianne tried to
tell herself Gabriel McNeill was the same guy she'd
worked for at Birdsong. The one she'd teased and
shoulder-bumped. The one who could raise an old
building from the dead with his woodworking prow-
ess and—yes—talented hands. She trusted him
to protect her grandmother's things—and Nana
herself—while they were on their honeymoon.

"I do," she blurted at what seemed to be the right
time, although she had a moment's horror that the
clerk had asked Gabe to repeat the words and not her.

But no, he was asking Gabe the same questions
now.

The rings slid onto her finger. She placed a platinum band on Gabe's hand.

Their fingers interlaced afterward. She didn't
know if she'd initiated that or Gabe had, but she
didn't want to let go. His nearness bolstered her when
she was feeling nervous. Weird, because he was half
the reason she felt nervous in the first place. But she
couldn't shake the comfort she took in his presence
after the working relationship they'd developed. She
hoped she didn't mess up that friendship by marrying him.

"You may kiss the bride." The words intruded on her frenzy of worries. It was the first truly clear message that had gotten through to her brain in the past fifteen minutes.

Kiss. The. Bride.

Each word echoed in slow motion in Brianne's mind. She watched Gabe's response to them, seeing the way he smiled at the representative from the clerk's office and then turned his full attention back to her.

The heat in his midnight blue eyes burned away everything else: the quiet of the room as a handful of people watched them, Jason with his distinctive baby sounds squealing over something. All of it seemed to happen elsewhere as Gabe wrapped his strong hands around her waist.

His touch warmed her right through two layers of lace and silk. Her senses swirled as he lowered his head toward hers, just the same way it had happened in countless forbidden fantasies. Her eyelids fluttered. She might have swayed on her feet.

The man had her spellbound.

Suspense killing her, she couldn't wait another moment or she risked swooning in his arms like a starry-eyed teenager. She clutched the lapels of his dark gray suit, anchoring herself upright. Tilting her face, she brushed her mouth to his in the barest imitation of a kiss. But before she could ease away, Gabe's fingers splayed wider on her back, spanning more of her spine as he drew her fully against him.

Heat scorched through her. His lips claimed hers, and he kissed her like he had all the time in the world to show her how rewarding being Mrs. Gabe Mc-Neill could be.

Seven

The kiss was meant to seal the deal. As a bonus, Gabe thought the contact might awaken his bride to the idea that physical intimacy could be a source of tremendous pleasure for them both.

What he hadn't bargained on was how much the feel of her lips would sear straight through his carefully laid plans to set his own body on fire. Brianne's fingers flexed against his chest, her nails lightly scoring his jacket before she pulled him tighter against her.

For a moment, he ignored everything else. While the witnesses held their collective breaths, Gabe deepened the kiss, taking the full taste of Brianne that he'd secretly craved from the first time they'd met. He sipped and savored her, letting the minty hesitation of her tongue melt away beneath his. The flavor of her raced through his bloodstream like a direct injection.

Off to Gabe's side, he heard a discreet cough followed by the clearing of a throat. The celebrant, he realized dimly, giving him a cue.

Reluctantly, Gabe pulled away from his new wife. His one consolation was watching her eyelids flutter open slowly, and her lips part in surprise.

As Nadine and the rest of their witnesses applauded, Gabe wanted to whisk away his bride with a fierceness that surprised him. The attraction felt like a fire suddenly exposed to oxygen. It whooshed around him so fast he wondered if it had singed his eyebrows.

"Congratulations, Mr. McNeill," the official from the clerk's office said as he packed up his book and paperwork. "I'll leave a copy of the marriage certificate with you."

Gabe took another moment to pull away his eyes from Brianne's dazed brown gaze.

"Of course." He passed the man a check and tried to run through his mental checklist of things to do before he and Brianne boarded their private flight to Cheyenne.

"May I take a photo, Mr. McNeill?" one of the maids asked as she shook Brianne's hand.

The woman was already holding up her phone. In fact, Gabe had asked her to quietly submit a story to the tabloid of her choice to make a little extra money on the side. She'd only accepted once he convinced her she could give the fee to a charity of her choice. Apparently, Ian's wife worked closely with a single mothers' charity and the maid had agreed it would be a worthy place to contribute the funds.

Beside him, Brianne reached for her bouquet for their photo, her eyes a little glazed and shell-shocked. He understood the feeling. Because even though they'd wed for practical purposes, they had still changed their lives forever. Nadine brought over Jason and handed the baby to him for the picture. His son wore a baby version of a tux, although the bow tie was simply sewn onto the cotton shirt.

"I would be glad to have a copy of the photo," Gabe told the maid, drawing Brianne closer for a picture he knew would be circulating online before they landed in Wyoming tonight.

Automatically, Brianne kissed Jason's head as she tipped her temple closer to the boy, reminding Gabe how connected the two of them had become these last ten months. Jason adored her. Was it so wrong of Gabe to want that strong feminine presence in the boy's life? There was no denying Brianne had an ease with the child and she seemed as smitten with Jason as he was with her.

"I need to speak to you privately," Brianne whispered while the woman snapped a few photos of the three of them. "It's urgent."

"Of course. I've already paid the clerk and we have the license. The violinist is packing up. We're all finished here." Gabe handed Jason back to Nadine so the boy could have his nap. Gabe was only too happy to have an excuse to disband the small group assembled to witness the wedding so he could speak to her alone. But her tone concerned him. "Is everything all right?" he asked as they strode out of the living room and into a small butler's pantry nearby.

"No." She shook her head, her beautiful dark hair shimmering in the overhead lights as they stood in the tight space full of floor-to-ceiling gray cabinets. "I spoke to Nana just before the ceremony and she said Wendy has been stealing from her and that we need to take precautions before my stepmother empties the whole house."

Gabe resisted the urge to swear. Barely.

"I'll call the police." He withdrew his phone from the pocket of his jacket.

"No. Nana asked me not to." Brianne put her hand over his to stop him, her touch reminding him how good she'd felt in his arms. "I wondered if we could have the place cleaned out and Nana's things put into storage until we move to Martinique."

He took a moment to absorb Brianne's words since the rest of him was all about the feel of her touch. Her gaze held his for a moment before she went to pull away her hand. He prevented her from moving too far, linking their fingers instead while that crackle of awareness fired through him.

"If that's really what you prefer." He nodded, remembering a conversation he'd had with Damon earlier in the day. "When Damon was staying in New York, he had a couple of bodyguards from a security firm that specializes in privacy and protection."

They were based in Silicon Valley, close to where Damon lived these days, but Gabe was familiar with the group from his time out there working on their software start-up. And they had a branch in New York. "I can get a couple of guys over there today, I'm sure."

"Would you?" Her fingers brushed the back of his hand, her pink diamond wedding ring glinting. She swayed ever so slightly toward him.

"I'll make it my top priority and call now." He was glad to do this for her, considering the way he was leaking the marriage news without telling her.

"Thank you." She squeezed his wrist. "So much."

"Of course. Brianne, we're married now. I'll do whatever I can to make your life easier and happier." It wasn't a declaration of love, but after the hellish experience he'd had with marriage, this was a vow that he meant. One he would keep. He already cared about Brianne deeply, so it was a pleasure to repay her for all the ways she'd been a good friend to him and to his son. "Do you think you can be ready to leave in another hour?"

"Easily. I've got a bag packed. I just need to get out of this dress." Letting go of him, she stared down at the close fitting minidress and the matching long jacket. "It's only got a million buttons up the back."

He couldn't imagine a better reason to delay their flight. Visions of helping Brianne out of her lace dress turned the air sultry in the narrow butler's pantry.

He lowered his voice, speaking close to her ear. "Once again, my services are at your disposal."

She glanced up fast. "That wasn't what I meant."

There was a hint of wariness in her tone. But there was something else, too. Awareness? Curiosity? Perhaps the kiss had sparked a new hunger in her, too. There'd always been the possibility of more simmering under the surface of their friendship.

"And yet think how much time it will save you if I get the top few buttons started." He reached around her and pushed some of her hair from the center of her back, feeling the warmth of her skin through the layers of lace. "I can unfasten a few, and then you can put the jacket back on so no one will know they're undone when you walk to your room. You can go through the kitchen, if you want, but I think the living room will be empty in another minute."

Lips pursed, she seemed to think it over.

Then, slowly, she turned around, presenting him with her back. Shrugging the lace jacket partially off her shoulders, she let the fabric catch at her elbows so that the top of her dress was exposed.

His heart rate accelerated.

He could lock the doors on either end of the narrow pantry and have guaranteed privacy. Instead, he simply slid a finger beneath the collar of the white lace dress and lifted it away from her warm skin. He used a thumb to push the first button back through the loop, freeing it. Then he repeated the action with another and another, revealing a narrow patch of bronzed skin between her shoulder blades.

He leaned closer, breathing in the scent of her soap and floral shampoo while she couldn't see him.

Tucking his fingers deeper in the dress, he let his knuckles brush her skin for a moment. Then they grazed the silk of her undergarments—the stiff strap of the bra that kept her lush curves in place.

"That's good," she said hastily, stepping forward so fast he nearly pulled off a button accidentally. "Thank you."

She kept her back turned for another moment as she shrugged into the matching lace jacket again.

Gabe's heart pounded so hard he was about to get light-headed in another minute. Touching her at all had been a bonus, he reminded himself.

"The car will be here at three o'clock to take us to the airport," he told her, his voice rough with unfulfilled want.

"I'll be ready." She glanced over her shoulder, her cheeks flushed and her eyes bright.

He'd bet her heart was hammering, too. Knowing that made him all the more ready to start the honeymoon.

Four hours and sixteen hundred miles later, Brianne still couldn't get Gabe's touch off her mind.

They disembarked in a private airfield north of Cheyenne, Wyoming, to a bitter wind that left her breathless. When they were in New York, she'd accepted a wool coat left behind by a guest of the McNeills, and now she clutched the long, dark cape tighter as Gabe guided her toward the hulking black SUV waiting nearby with its lights on. Because of the time difference, it was still daylight here. The airstrip was so deserted it looked like an open field except for the two lit runways and one small metal hangar. Snow swirled around her feet like a fluffy tornado, the white crystalline flakes glinting like the facets of her pink diamond as they swirled.

And even in that shock of cold whipping off the nearby mountains, Brianne's skin still warmed automatically when her husband touched her through heavy wool, the sensory memory of what had happened in the butler's pantry heating a shivery path down her spine.

The driver from the Range Rover sprinted past them to take a rolling cart of bags off the plane. The man wore a parka so big his head looked unnaturally small even with a knit hat pulled low on his head. She seriously envied the coat, even with the warmth of Gabe's leather glove splayed between her shoulder blades.

"Are you warm enough?" he asked in her right ear, his voice triggering another sensual flashback to their time in the butler's pantry.

She was getting used to the tone he used only for her.

His wife.

His *second* wife, now that she thought about it. Had he even bothered to warn Theresa that he was getting remarried? The thought threatened to take Brianne's legs out from under her faster than the slippery ice as they crossed the tarmac.

"I think it's the wind more than the cold." She half

shouted to be heard, the gusts blowing past her ear hard enough to make a high-pitched howl.

Without slowing his step, he raised the shawl-like hood on the cape and twined the ends around her neck to secure it. The movement sent a quick smattering of snowflakes into her hair, but the fabric quickly blocked the wind around her ears.

If only he could solve her other worry as easily. Would Jason's mother resent her fiercely for marrying Gabe? Or might Gabe be honest with her about their reasons for the wedding? She needed to ask him about it.

A moment later, they were in the back of the Range Rover and the driver had the bags loaded. Once they were underway and she'd thawed out a little, she lowered the hood and peered out the window into the swirl of white snow.

"I feel like we're in the middle of nowhere." There weren't many vehicles on the road. "It's like driving in a white vacuum."

More than that, being at Gabe's side in the lonesome emptiness only enhanced the urge to wrap herself around him. She felt like they could be the last two people on earth out here.

"I spent a lot of time on the plane looking into places for us to stay, but in the end, I think it will be easiest to take a cabin on a hobby ranch my grandfather has rented for his stay out here." Gabe pressed a button on his phone and showed her a map. "This pin is the ranch."

"Wait a second." She straightened and edged back

Dear Reader,

IT'S A FACT: if you answer 4 quick questions, we'll send you 4 FREE REWARDS!

I'm not kidding you. As a leading publisher of women's fiction, we value your opinions... and your time. That's why we are prepared to **reward** you handsomely for completing our mini-survey. In fact, we have 4 Free Rewards for you, including 2 free books and 2 free gifts.

As you may have guessed, that's why our mini-survey is called **"4 for 4"**. Answer 4 questions and get 4 Free Rewards. It's that simple!

Thank you for participating in our survey,

Pam Powers

To get your 4 FREE REWARDS:
Complete the survey below and return the insert today to receive 2 FREE BOOKS and 2 FREE GIFTS guaranteed!

"4 for 4" MINI-SURVEY

1 Is reading one of your favorite hobbies?
☐ YES ☐ NO

2 Do you prefer to read instead of watch TV?
☐ YES ☐ NO

3 Do you read newspapers and magazines?
☐ YES ☐ NO

4 Do you enjoy trying new book series with FREE BOOKS?
☐ YES ☐ NO

YES! I have completed the above Mini-Survey. Please send me my 4 FREE REWARDS (worth over $20 retail). I understand that I am under no obligation to buy anything, as explained on the back of this card.

225/326 HDL GMYG

FIRST NAME	LAST NAME

ADDRESS

APT.#	CITY

STATE/PROV.	ZIP/POSTAL CODE

READER SERVICE—Here's how it works:

to get a better look. "Did you say he rented a *whole ranch*? For himself?"

"He's had one of his grandsons here with him on and off as he waits for his estranged son to see him." Gabe leaned deeper into the leather seat beside her, his arm stretched along the back of her headrest. "So he hasn't been totally alone. He travels with a personal assistant and a medical caretaker, too, so he needs room for a few staffers."

Just when she thought she had a handle on this family's wealth and lifestyle, something else made her jaw drop.

"And now we'll stay with him, too?" She told herself that was a good thing since being alone with Gabe for a honeymoon—no matter how much of a pretense their marriage was—could only lead to temptation.

"Not in the same building, just on the same property." He pointed toward the phone again. "The red pin is the main ranch house. This blue dot is the guest cottage." He skimmed his finger west on the map a bit, a distance the scale showed to be a mile or two. "I thought we'd be more comfortable there. It's got maid service and I messaged the caretaker to stock the fridge, so they're expecting us. But it's not too late to book a hotel, or a house of our own, if you prefer."

Of course it wasn't too late. The man had arranged a wedding with a day's notice.

"The cottage sounds great." She tried to smile to show this was all fine by her. But the reality of this being her honeymoon night was sinking in fast. Even now, Gabe's gloved fingers toyed with a lock of her hair, igniting fresh shivers.

And still she hadn't asked him what his ex-wife thought about their marriage. Or if he'd told her at all. Brianne had never formed much of a relationship with the woman other than saying hello in passing and having one conversation about what flowers hummingbirds liked best. Unlike Gabe, Theresa had always viewed Brianne as a domestic—a staff member whose sole function was to keep her employer happy.

"Are you worried about anything?" Gabe returned the phone to the pocket of his camel-colored overcoat. "Have you been getting regular updates on your grandmother?"

"She's fine, thank you. And yes, Adella has been great about sending me messages." Brianne appreciated his thoughtfulness.

Still, it was difficult to think about anything else beyond the fact that she was heading to a remote Wyoming retreat to spend her wedding night with Gabe. No matter that he'd agreed not to press the attraction between them, the possibility of something happening loomed large in her thoughts.

"And the security team I hired to clean out your grandmother's apartment is still uploading the photos of the contents."

"No hurry. I'm just glad to know Wendy won't be able to take anything else." She'd been researching touristy things to do near Cheyenne, Wyoming, about an hour before their flight landed, when Gabe had let her know Nana's apartment had been secured and her things successfully moved out. "I'm most curious about what she's been hiding in the broom closet."

She'd shared the secret of Nana's hiding place with Gabe, of course, so he could relay the information to the team he'd sent into the Brooklyn apartment. Not that she believed her grandmother owned anything very valuable in the financial sense. But there was a nostalgic value to anything that was important to Rose, and Brianne wanted to be sure nothing was left behind when she relocated her to Martinique.

"When we're settled in the cottage, I'll check the link again and see what new photos are up so you can go through them." His arm shifted from the headrest to slide around her shoulders. "Something else is bothering you, though. I can tell."

Two things, actually.

It seemed easier to admit her worries about his ex than to confess her other fear: that she wouldn't be able to keep her hands off him once they were settled into some romantic honeymoon suite in the middle of nowhere. The fact that she kept replaying the feel of his hands on her back when he'd unbuttoned her wedding dress sure didn't inspire confidence in her ability to keep things platonic.

"There is something." She knew his ex was a sore subject, so she took a deep breath before she blurted, "Did you warn Theresa we were getting married?"

He tensed beside her. The reaction was immediate and reminded Brianne how much emotion he still had invested in that broken relationship.

"No," he admitted stiffly, straightening in his seat as the Range Rover pulled off the main road onto a rough rural lane. "Our relationship is not her concern. And especially not on our wedding day."

Right. Except that he'd married Theresa because he'd loved her.

As for Brianne?

She was his means to an end.

And if that didn't put a damper on the hot, sensual desire she'd been feeling for Gabe, she didn't know what would. Before she could argue the point, however, the big SUV lurched to a stop in front of a big, Craftsman-style home with well-lit windows looking into cozy rooms with pine-log walls and rafters.

Her only consolation in seeing the snow-swept winter retreat was that maybe resisting Gabe tonight would be easier with the subject of his ex a newly raw ache between them.

Eight

He simply needed to regroup.

After his misstep with Brianne in the Range Rover, he'd sensed her retreat. When they'd entered the cabin, she'd slipped away to unpack at the earliest opportunity. In theory, he understood why she would have preferred that he warn his ex-wife about their new marriage. That would have been kinder, perhaps. But it hadn't occurred to him since his parting with Theresa had been acrimonious at every turn, despite his best efforts to make it easy for her to see Jason and maintain a relationship with their son.

Yes, he'd taken steps to ensure his ex-wife found out about the marriage to Brianne. But no doubt the pictures leaked to the tabloids weren't the method Brianne would have chosen. So now, he was regrouping to salvage his honeymoon and make amends with his new bride, a woman he did not wish to hurt. Brianne was different from his ex in every way, and she deserved his best efforts in this marriage, even if their reasons for the union had been practical and not romantic.

Gabe set the timer on the oven to remind himself to flip the steaks and mentally ran through his dinner preparations. He had the candles lit in the dining room, but he'd laid a fire in the huge stone hearth in the living room if she preferred to eat there. The wine had been chilled before they arrived, but he'd opened it to breathe. He'd put a loaf of fresh bread in the warming drawer, and tossed some salads. In a moment of optimism, he'd even switched on the heat for the outdoor hot tub on the master bedroom balcony in case he could convince Brianne to join him after dinner.

Now he needed to make amends to her. Steer the talk away from conversational powder kegs and focus on all the positive things that this marriage meant for both of them. Health care and stability for her aging grandparent. Securing Jason's place in Malcolm McNeill's powerful family. And, if he could convince her to follow the attraction that had long been simmering between them, a tremendous amount of pleasure.

Turning off the broiler, he left the oven door slightly open and went upstairs to call Brianne down for the meal. He passed wall after wall of darkened glass, since the sun had set here even though they'd gained a couple of hours on the day by flying west. The house would feel like a fishbowl anywhere else but not in this remote corner of the world, where there was nothing else around them for miles. Although the place was part of the larger ranch his grandfather had rented for the month, they couldn't see any other outbuildings from here.

"Dinner is ready," he announced outside her bedroom door. He'd tried to talk her into taking the master suite, but she'd been quietly adamant when they first arrived, making herself at home in the second bedroom on the upper floor.

He rapped on the solid pine door now, and it swung open at his touch. Light spilled from the room.

"Brianne?" He didn't want to intrude, but maybe she'd decided to nap.

Or shower.

A surge of awareness crackled across his skin as he was overcome with memories of kissing her during their wedding. Unbuttoning her afterward. As sensual encounters went, they were tame. Outwardly, they looked pretty innocent.

The effect on him, however, was anything but.

Striding inside the bedroom, he found no clues to her whereabouts. The white quilt on the huge bed was untouched except for the few clothes left scattered there. There were shopping bags on the floor from local stores that must have contained some of the winter items he'd ordered for her. The rental agency had said it would be no problem to rush-deliver hats, gloves and more outerwear along with some warm sweaters and slippers. Maybe not the height of fashion, but he knew Brianne wouldn't care.

Still, she deserved beautiful things. Seeing the unisex insulated gloves in different sizes made him all the more determined to indulge her. Hearing the stories about her stepmother had shed some light on the clothing choices Brianne made. Gabe had thought she dressed in cargo pants and T-shirts for work because they were functional for gardening. After meeting Wendy and learning about the way she'd made Brianne uncomfortable in her own skin as a child, he'd been angry. It explained a lot about the way his wife downplayed her beauty.

He was about to go back downstairs to search for her when something pelted the French door near him.

What the hell?

Turning, he thought maybe an icy branch had fallen from a tree to knock against the glass. But while he stared out the window, a blob of heavy snow hit the pane and slid down. This time, the sound was accompanied by muted feminine laughter.

A shadow moved outside the window on the second-floor balcony that wrapped around the whole back of the house. He reached back toward the bed long enough to jam a navy hat on his head and stuff his fingers into a pair of black Gore-Tex gloves. Charging outside, he faced the culprit head-on.

Brianne was busy scooping up another snowball, scraping red gloves through the foot of accumulation on the wooden deck. She'd traded her wool cape for a red down parka and boots. A gray knit cap was pulled low over her eyes, her ponytail covered with snow and hanging bedraggled over one shoulder.

His loafers would be ruined, but he had no intention of leaving the aggression unanswered, especially after he'd heard that laughter of hers. Had she moved on from their earlier disagreement? Or simply found an outlet for her frustration with him? He'd thought dinner would smooth things over between them, but if she preferred a snowy standoff, he was ready.

"I'd think carefully about your next move," he warned her, taking in her pink cheeks and bright eyes as she stalked closer to him, the wind lifting her hair off her shoulder and whipping it across the front of her parka. "I can't very well lob snow missiles at my new bride, but I can get even other ways."

"You can't play that card." She wagged one gloved finger at him, her voice raised so he could hear her over the howl of the wind. "No veiled threats allowed, Mr. McNeill. I give you my permission to get into an old-fashioned snowball fight with me."

He'd missed this part of their relationship. The teasing and one-upping. Only now, there was a new dimension to it thanks to their wedding vows. The possibility of things getting much more interesting.

"I'd hardly call it a veiled threat." He kept one eye on the snowball in her hand as they squared off a few feet apart in the middle of the balcony. "You make it sound ominous."

"Okay. No *mystery* threats, then. No suggestive innuendo allowed."

"I draw the line there, Mrs. McNeill." He liked

her expression as he tested out the new name. Even in the reflected light from the house, he could see a flare of something that looked like pleasure in her eyes. "Half the reason I married you was for the suggestive innuendo."

Her gaze narrowed as her fingers closed harder around the snowball. "Maybe I should have read that contract more carefully."

They both knew she'd read it exhaustively, working on a tentative draft while her grandmother was in the emergency room. She'd changed wording in a handful of places and argued against several points of the settlement to try and decrease the amount she would receive after they'd been married for a year. He'd tweaked the wording as she wished, but he'd left the settlement terms as generous as originally written.

"You didn't see the suggestive-language addendum?" He moved fractionally closer, ready to disarm her if the opportunity presented itself.

A light snow fell, or else the wind kicked up enough to make it feel like it was actively snowing. There was a swirl of white between them. Behind her, he could see the outline of the railing. Down on the far end of the balcony, he could see the shape of the hot tub he'd warmed up earlier. He shifted closer still.

"I know perfectly well there's no such thing. We're married for a handful of hours and we're already at odds about the agreement." She tsked and sighed dramatically.

"I'm the one who has come under attack, though." He nodded meaningfully toward the hand that still held the snowball. "Maybe I'd be more amenable if you put down your arms."

"And risk retribution?" She shook her head. "I'll go on firing, thank you very much."

"At such close range?" He put a hand to his chest. He only wore a sweater and a shirt in the chilly winter air, but the thought of touching Brianne heated him inside and out. "I don't think you can pull the trigger on your new groom, Brianne. Not when you know how much I'm dying for payback."

He closed the distance between them even more; they were so close his body blocked the snowflakes from landing on her. So close he could see her sway on her feet for a moment, as if she wanted to fall into his arms as much as he wanted her to.

Her eyelashes fluttered. She dragged in a slow breath.

And socked him square in the chest with the snowball.

Leaping back with a squeal of delight, she grinned at him, delighted with herself.

He was nothing less than delighted with her, too. He didn't think twice about going after her, wrapping his arms around her from behind and plunging them both into the snowdrift built up against one side of the balcony.

Rolling himself in a way that he fell first, he cushioned her fall with his body. The shock of cold against his back was a minor inconvenience for the reward of having her curves pressed snug to the front of him, her wiggling weight a delectable and unexpected treat.

She laughed herself breathless, her breasts brushing his hands where he held her around her ribs. He battled the desire to slide his palms under the parka, since that would only make her cold.

It wasn't that bad out, he decided. Midforties, maybe. And although he was lying in the snow, at least the drift blocked the wind coming off the mountains. He could lie there a little longer. Especially if he got her turned around.

Gently, he rocked her sideways, putting enough space between them to spin her in his arms as he moved her so they ended up nose-to-nose.

"You're insane," she accused softly, her breath a warm huff on his cheek. "You don't even have a coat on."

He kept his lower arm pillowing his head and hers. "I've never met a nicer way to stay warm." He used his free hand to pluck a few icy strands of her hair from her cheek and set them behind her.

"We should go inside," she insisted, her expression turning more serious. "It's cold out here."

"I'm taking my payback." He watched her while the words sank in.

He heard the hitch in her breathing. Saw the wordless movement of her lips as she thought through whatever argument that wasn't going to fly.

Then her teeth sank into her lower lip and he would swear she was biting back a smile.

"Is it too late for me to give in gracefully?" she asked, edging closer to him in the mound of snow, her hips sealing tighter to his.

Adrenaline surged through him so fast he knew he could consummate the whole wedding night right here if she wanted him to.

"It's definitely not too late." He cupped her shoulder to pull her against him. "Tell me, wife." He let the word hang between them, tasting it on his tongue the way he wanted to taste her again. "How are you going to make it up to me?"

Brianne had been deluding herself to think anything would keep her away from Gabe tonight.

She'd instigated the snowball fight in a misguided attempt to return to the playfulness of their relationship from years past. Thinking about Gabe's ex had made her doubt herself and her hasty decision to wed. She'd been longing to return to more comfortable terrain with him, where they could tease one another and have fun.

But of course that had been naive. Or maybe subconsciously she'd just been trying to push past the discomfort of his ex-wife's shadow over this day. Either way, Brianne gulped in breaths of the thin mountain air, hoping to cool the fire in her belly. A fire that leaped higher the more Gabe touched her.

"I can make it up to you by cooking dinner," she offered, out of her element when it came to flirting.

"I already prepared the meal." He shrugged a shoulder like he had all the time in the world to wade through this dilemma, when here he was lying in a snowbank with just a shirt and a sweater between his skin and the frosty white powder. "That's not going to work."

Her cheek rested on his arm, its muscle warm and strong beneath the cashmere and wool. Her breasts were pressed to his chest, causing a pleasurable ache as his gloved hand stroked up her spine through her parka.

"I could dry your clothes for you since it's my fault you got plastered with a well-aimed snowball." She strived to keep things light, knowing she was swimming against the current with all the sparks streaking between them. But it was better than being over her head.

"Now we're getting somewhere." He nodded his satisfaction at the plan. "I can't wait for you to start undressing me."

She opened her mouth to argue and realized she had no comeback. Not while her brain got busy supplying mental pictures of her tunneling her hands under his sweater. Unbuttoning the fastenings on his shirt. Splaying her fingers over the sculpted torso she'd ogled on more than one occasion.

"I'm going to let you in on a secret that may surprise you." She tipped her head to his chest for a moment, feeling awkward, then telling herself to get over it. Lifting her face to his again, she blurted, "I'm not all that experienced with men."

He didn't appear terribly surprised. He peered down at her, his blue eyes intent. Thoughtful.

"Does it make you uncomfortable when I talk about you undressing me?" he asked.

A shiver went through her.

"Um. Not exactly." She tried to identify what it made her feel. "I would say I'm intrigued, but possibly ill-prepared."

"Intrigued is good." The smile he gave her inspired another shiver. "But you're starting to get cold. I think we should move this discussion to the hot tub." He pointed to the other end of the snow-covered balcony.

"There's a hot tub?" Sure enough, she could make out the shape of it, a chunky rectangle with blue lights around the rim barely visible under a cover of some kind.

"I turned the heat on in the sauna next to it, and put robes and towels inside." He sat up, bringing her with him. "You can change in there and meet me in the tub."

"Where are you going?" She stood with his help.

"I'd like to see what I can salvage of dinner so we have something to eat afterward." Giving her a gentle push in one direction, he moved in the other. "Go warm up and I'll be there in a minute."

Brianne headed to the wooden hut at the end of the house, ducked through the cedar door into the fragrant heat of the sauna and closed the insulated entrance behind her. She ignored the light switch, able to see well enough in the glow of coals in the fire box. She peeled off her coat, hat and gloves, then piled them on a built-in bench. After spotting

the thick white spa robes, she tugged off her sweater
and jeans, but left her underwear on since she had
no bathing suit. She gave herself another minute to
warm up in the dry heat before throwing on a robe
and darting back out into the snow.

Squealing at the feel of snow on her bare feet, she
padded through it fast and climbed two steps to the
hot tub. After lifting off the heavy leather cover and
folding it in half, she unfastened her robe at warp
speed, tossing it on the cover and sinking down into
the bubbling spa.

She had just closed her eyes and settled into one
of the molded seats covered in jets when she heard
Gabe's footsteps on the balcony.

Was he naked? She wondered, but she didn't cheat
and open her eyes. Well, not until it was too late to
tell for sure. By the time she peeked at him sidelong,
all she saw was a glimpse of his bare chest disap-
pearing down into the water. A tantalizing hint of
corded muscle as steam rose all around him.

"That feels amazing." He tipped his head back on
the headrest beside hers, and their shoulders brushed.

Awareness crackled to life.

"I've never moved so fast as I did between the
sauna and the tub." She stared at his profile illumi-
nated in the ambient light from the house.

She still couldn't believe she'd married him today.
The ceremony had been a blur, with her mind on
her grandmother's health and the news about her
stepmother pilfering things from Rose's few possessions. But the marriage felt real enough now, as

she sat mostly naked at Gabe's side in the middle of nowhere. Snow swirled just above her nose, most of it melting before it landed.

"I brought some wine." He pried open an eyelid and reached behind him to retrieve an open bottle on the step. "It might warm you up on the inside."

Also, it might help with the nervous butterflies she had about her wedding night.

"Sure." She reached behind him to retrieve the bottle and a glass. "I'll pour while you warm up, though. I'm still feeling a little guilty for luring you out into the frigid temperatures without your jacket."

"It's not really that cold out." He watched her pour the first glass and handed her the second. "And you have no reason to feel guilty when we already agreed that payback is forthcoming."

Setting the wine on the step outside the tub, Brianne sat sideways in her seat to face him, the hot bubbles bursting all around her shoulders as air injectors worked their magic.

"Since it's our honeymoon and all, maybe you'll feel compelled to grant clemency." She sipped the wine and appreciated the subtle heat it put in her veins.

"I do owe you a wedding gift." He tipped his glass to hers even though she'd already stolen a sip. After the gentle clink, he raised the cut crystal. "Here's to marrying my best friend."

A ripple of unexpected pleasure that he would call her that went through her.

"Cheers." She lifted her glass and drank to the toast, feeling the weight of his gaze on her the whole time.

The nerve endings all along her arms and shoulders went haywire, making goose bumps appear.

"I didn't think about a wedding gift for you," she admitted, setting aside the glass on one of the drink platforms along the outside edge of the tub.

The curtain of hazy snow and steam around them gave the sense that they were all alone in the world, a veil of cold mist separating them from everything but one another.

Or maybe the wine was going to her head. She felt a sweet happiness all over to be with Gabe. It was dangerous, perhaps, to feel that way. But she'd never been with a man like him, someone strong and noble, kind and warmhearted.

And so very sexy.

Her eyes dipped to the top of his chest above the water as he drained his glass and set it aside, his triceps flexing in a way that made her want to take a bite.

"I certainly didn't expect a wedding gift." He shook his head, a wry smile kicking up one side of his mouth. "We'll have to make our own rules for this marriage since the regular conventions aren't going to apply."

"Like tonight, for example." She hadn't meant to say it out loud, but there it was, floating on the cold breeze before she could take it back. Drawing a steadying breath, she explained herself. "I don't need to worry about your expectations because—"

"Because there are none." He cupped her shoulders with his hands, a warm weight that anchored her in the swirling water. "I thought we deserved this time together to get to know each other as more than friends, but I will be glad just to talk to you tonight. To learn how to make you happy."

"I know that." She wanted to close her eyes and concentrate on how his hands felt on her. To soak up all the sensations of being with him. "You never made me feel like you brought me here for more than that, but still…it's a wedding night. I can't deny I've been thinking about the possibilities of what that means."

His thumbs skated a slow circle over the tops of her shoulders, a subtle touch that set the rest of her on fire.

"I've been doing plenty of thinking of my own," he admitted. "But that doesn't mean we have to act on it."

If he kept touching her, though, the possibility of her launching across the hot tub to kiss him was very real.

"When I said I wasn't all that experienced, I didn't mean to suggest I've never been with a guy. Of course I have." Though she had kept her virginity longer than any of her friends, haunted by her stepmother's taunts long after they should have lost their power to hurt her. "I just don't feel like I ever got high marks. You know?"

"Sex shouldn't be a graded assignment." He said it with one-hundred-percent seriousness.

But she laughed anyway, because it was a strange conversation for a wedding night. "Right. I get that." She flipped a damp piece of hair out of her eyes as she warmed to the discussion. "But when I decided to lose my virginity, I think I was probably...too determined. I did some research and felt well-prepared, but in the end—epic fail." She shook her head, remembering the expression on her boyfriend's face afterward. It hadn't been blissful pleasure.

More like being shell-shocked, maybe.

"The thought of you researching to the point of being overprepared is going to animate some very good dreams for me." He never stopped touching her. His thumbs trailed down the satin straps of her bra in the back. Then in the front. Over and over. "It's my turn to be intrigued."

"I think I was studying techniques that were too advanced for a beginner." She shrugged, the water around her splashing with the movement. "But I don't like looking foolish, and I'd waited so long to give sex a try that I put a lot of pressure on myself not to make it obvious that I was a first-timer."

"What about afterward?" Gabe's knee grazed hers under the water and she didn't skitter away because it felt too good. "Didn't things get better once the first time was out of the way?"

"I wasn't keen to repeat the experiment at the time." She retrieved her wineglass and took another small sip. "But now, I think maybe I'd like to."

Nine

Go slow.

Gabe repeated the mantra to himself, waiting to move—waiting to breathe—until he was certain his revved-up body got the message. He bit the inside of his cheek and focused on the sting because he sure as hell wasn't going to ruin Brianne's *second* time. The pressure was on to make sure the night was perfect after the first experience had underwhelmed her so thoroughly she hadn't cared to try again.

Until now.

It was the "until now" that made him hunger to bury himself inside her. Show her how pleased it made him that she'd chosen him even after whatever had happened that first time. He breathed deep, more turned on than he'd ever been and knowing he couldn't act on it. Yet. Or at least not the way he wanted to.

Go slow.

"How about we start with a kiss?" His gaze lowered to her delectable mouth.

With his fingers curved around her shoulders, he could feel her quick intake of breath. The trip of her pulse under the heel of his hand.

She shifted closer to him in the swirling water, her knee pressing higher on his thigh as she repositioned herself. Then she raised her hands to his face, her damp fingers sliding along his jaw.

Gazes locked, he watched her until the last moment, when the feel of her lips sent a bolt of heat up his spine. She tasted like cabernet and snowflakes, sexy and innocent at the same time. Unbidden visions of her researching "advanced" sex techniques flickered across his mind's eye.

Go slow.

Shoving the wild imaginings out of his head, he tipped her chin up to kiss his way down her delicate throat. Her skin was hot despite the cold night air and the flurries that were gaining momentum. She smelled like exotic flowers, like the gardens she coaxed out of the earth. He inhaled the fragrance, stronger behind one ear, and combed his fingers through the damp hair falling out of the haphazard clasp.

Brianne gripped his forearms and pulled herself so close she was half-sprawled across his lap. Having her hip nudge his erection was not helping the go-slow approach. Her breasts pressing against his chest fulfilled several of his fantasies, and he did everything he could do not to peel off the satin cups of her bra to feel all of her. Instead, he gently nipped her neck. Her ear. Her fingers splayed wider on his chest, her touches more urgent as she arched to give him better access.

He took his time kissing places along her collarbone and shoulder, licking a path under the bra strap until she raked both satin strips down herself.

"I want more than kisses," she demanded suddenly, her dark eyes blazing with a new fire he could see even out here, under the stars. "I am ready."

He reminded himself that her idea of being ready for more probably wasn't the same as his. But he gladly took the opportunity to flick open the clasp of the satin bra and let it float away on a tide of bubbles. She filled his hands and then some, her softness making him impossibly harder. When she arched her back, her breasts lifted out of the water, rivulets streaking down her skin as he bent to kiss first one taut peak and then the other. She rocked against his lap, her throaty moan a plea for more that he damn well wanted to give her.

"We should go inside." He gauged the distance from the tub to the bed in the master suite, just on the other side of the sliding glass door nearby.

"I'm having fun, though," she whispered in his ear, her lips lingering to kiss him there. "I hate to stop."

"It'll only be for a minute." He wanted her in

bed, where she would be most comfortable. If Brianne's second time was going to happen, he wasn't going to risk a hot-tub encounter. "If you stand up, I'll wrap that robe around you and have you inside before you can blink."

She glanced over her shoulder and nodded, grinning with a playful sexiness. "Okay. If you insist."

Springing out of the water, she wrapped her arms around herself while he lunged for the robe to cover her. He moved the wine bottle off the steps and then bounded out of the tub himself before plucking her off her feet and carrying her inside. Her light laughter revved him higher, assuring him she was fully on board with his haste. What an incredible surprise this woman was turning out to be.

He toed the French door closed with one foot while he carried her into the master bathroom, setting her on the tiled surround of the raised garden tub. Still in his cotton boxers, he was dripping water everywhere. He took two towels off the warmer near the shower and handed her one, keeping the other to dry himself off. He dug another towel out of the closet to throw on the floor so she didn't slip.

"How was that?" He watched her wring out her long hair and then dab it dry.

"Getting out of the water wasn't nearly as bad as when I went in. I'm warmer now." She set aside the towel and turned dark eyes toward him. "And less nervous. Thank you for that."

He wrapped his towel around his waist and pulled her to her feet. "I'm glad you relaxed."

"It helped to feel like I warned you." Her wry smile, he now knew, hid an old hurt.

He planned to do whatever he could to heal that. Now, and every other night they were together. Tipping her chin up, he grazed her lips with his and breathed her in.

"I should warn you, too." He tunneled his fingers through her thick, damp hair. "You're going to forget everything that came before tonight."

Folding her in his arms, he kissed her, and it was better than all the times he'd secretly thought about it. He could taste her passion, and she met his hunger with a new need of her own.

She wrapped her arms around his neck, arching against him, and it wasn't enough. He carried her to the bed, making sure she stayed in the moment with him, very ready to make good on his promise to her. He could tell from the kisses that this was going to be better than anything he'd ever imagined. Anything he'd ever dreamed.

He laid her in the center of the bed. Her dark eyes were bright with passion, her hair spilling in every direction on the starched white pillowcase. He stripped off his towel and boxers and she surprised him by shrugging out of her robe and wriggling out of her panties. She lay before him, gloriously naked, and for a moment, he could only stare. His mouth went dry, and his body ached for her with a desperation he'd never felt for another woman.

"Please." Her voice was ragged as she lifted a hand to reach for him. "Don't stop."

Her touch, just a sweep of her knuckles along his chest, propelled him forward. He joined her on the bed, rolling her to her side, her skin like silk against him. A sigh of satisfaction hissed from between his lips, and he thought he heard a soft moan of pleasure from her at the same moment.

Finally.

He sketched a caress down her spine, waiting for his heartbeat to steady. Brianne was having none of it, though. She wriggled closer, raining kisses along his chest. Curving a hand around her hip, he cupped the heat between her thighs. She made a hungry sound, her head falling back on the pillow, her beautiful breasts drawing even with his mouth.

Unable to resist, he licked his way along the tight peaks and sank his finger deep inside her. She wrapped herself around him, legs and arms, giving herself to him. He took his time, loving the feel of her. Learning the touches she liked best until her hips arched and her breath caught.

She came apart in his arms in a rush of heat, her whole body shuddering with her completion. He held her, stroking her while her body quaked, then kissed her neck when she quieted.

Brianne waited for her breathing to return to normal. The orgasm was an amazing—and generous—surprise. She hadn't been expecting it and now she felt a heady pleasure streaking through her veins, making her feel boneless with sensual bliss.

A bliss Gabe had delivered with ease and—judging

by the erection nudging her thighs—considerable pleasure. Seized with the need to give him every bit as much fulfillment in return, she remembered the research she'd done before her first time.

She felt compelled to apply the teachings now.

Except he was already palming a condom.

"Gabe?" She wrapped her hand around his, halting his movement. "I'd love to repay the favor in kind." She meant it. Her pulse quickened. "I want you to feel as good as I do right now and, as I mentioned, I did study how to—"

He kissed her until she all but forgot what she'd been about to say.

"I will enjoy that even more when I have some restraint left." His words were a warm vibration against her ear. "I can't hold back much longer, Brianne."

A thrill shot through her and she let go of his wrist, ready for whatever he wanted next. She sensed that when he pleased himself he was going to please her, too.

Still, the thought didn't prepare her for the feel of him between her thighs. Pressing. Filling. She wrapped her arms around his neck and hung on, her hips meeting his as he moved inside her. She'd dreamed about him often enough in the years she'd worked for him, but she'd never imagined being with him would be like this. Transporting. So good, her toes curled when she wrapped her legs around his waist to hold him tighter.

This time, there was no thinking. No research had been needed. Her body knew what it wanted.

Gabe.

Everywhere. Skin to skin. Flesh to flesh. Savoring the bristle of his chin, the calluses of his fingers, every nuance of this man.

She arched up to kiss him and found him staring down at her. His gaze locked on hers. They drew out the moment. Even as they moved together, driving each other higher, he leaned down to take her lips. Kiss her deeply.

That was when another wave of release hit her. Sweet spasms rocked her, again and again. She clung to Gabe, helpless while the sensations gripped her fiercely. She felt him go rigid moments later, heard his hoarse shout as he found that same completion.

Sometime afterward, when her heart had finally steadied, Gabe rolled her to his side, tucking her against him. A languid warmth persisted everywhere, her body tender with the newness of so much pleasure. She peeked at him through her lashes and saw him stretched beside her, his hand still curled possessively around her hip.

A swell of emotion rose in her chest and she tried not to notice it. Maybe she'd been wise to avoid sex since that first time. Maybe, deep down inside, she'd known that she was the kind of woman given to romantic longings and…whatever it was she was feeling for Gabe.

She couldn't afford to venture down that road with him, and she knew it. Gabe McNeill married her because they were friends. Because he trusted her not to fall in love with him or take advantage of his generous nature.

The latter part of that equation was simple, of course. She'd never want to hurt this man. But the sudden crushing weight on her chest told her how difficult it was going to be to keep her feelings on lockdown. Especially when the physical intimacy had the power to lay bare her emotions.

"Brianne." He spoke her name against her hair, making her realize he'd been watching her, too.

Turning her gaze up to meet his, she found a seriousness in his expression. Had he felt the same cataclysmic shift in their relationship that she had?

"Mmm?" She couldn't speak past the burn in her throat, afraid she would blurt out something unwise and far too revealing.

"Are you hungry? I can bring us dinner anytime." He stroked her hair, following the line of the waves that resulted from air-drying.

"I'm good for now." She didn't want to move. And, heaven help her, she wasn't ready for him to get up, either.

Maybe, if they waited long enough, the feelings would subside. All that churned-up emotion would simply settle back down into her being and sink beneath the surface, where she could manage it again. But then he tipped up her face to his, holding her steady while he looked into her eyes.

She felt herself falling in that blue gaze. Weightless, and with nothing to anchor her.

When he kissed her this time, the charge between

them was still electric, but it was stronger. Deeper. She reached for him hungrily, as if they hadn't just worn each other out with passion. He skimmed a touch up her hip, over her belly and breasts, and set her on fire again.

She couldn't get enough of him. Kissing, licking, tasting, touching. She needed him everywhere and he fulfilled her slightest desire as if they'd been made for one another. He slid into her once more. Slowly. Deliberately.

Breathless from the sensual heat, she gave herself to him completely. No defenses. It all happened so fast, there was no time to resurrect a single barrier between them.

When he drove them both over the edge this time, Brianne felt a piece of her heart give way, too.

Ten

When Brianne awoke the second time, the savory scent of dinner made her stomach growl. The bed beside her was empty, the sheets tangled around her legs. She checked her phone and it was only ten o'clock Wyoming time. That meant midnight for her body.

No wonder her stomach was rumbling.

Slipping on the fluffy white spa robe, she could hear Gabe moving around the kitchen downstairs. Cabinet doors closing. The clink of silverware and dishes. That he'd left her side to prepare them both a meal didn't surprise her. He'd always been warm-hearted. Thoughtful. So she wasn't foolish enough to think that dinner came as the result of any new tenderness toward her. Running her fingers through her tousled hair, she told herself to keep things light between them.

And guard the rest of her heart with a whole lot more vigilance.

She stopped by her bedroom for a pair of socks, then followed her nose through the airy Craftsman home. The walls were natural pine log in every room, but the modern furnishings kept the place contemporary. High ceilings and exposed rafters mingled with stainless-steel fixtures and gray twill seating brightened with punches of red or yellow, depending on the room.

There were paintings of Wyoming landscapes in all the rooms. She recognized the Devils Tower and Grand Tetons. As she reached the kitchen and the source of all the appealing scents, the paintings gave way to natural wood cabinets and a rounded island set for two, white tapers already burning. Gabe was pulling a broiler pan with two steaks out of the oven.

"Perfect timing." He grinned as he put the pan between the place settings on the island. Dressed in a pair of low-slung sweatpants and no shirt, he made her mouth water even more than the dinner. "The meat looks pretty good considering I had to warm it up a second time."

Tossing aside a pot holder, he leaned over to kiss her cheek and pull out one of the padded leather bar stools in front of the gray granite countertop. She closed her eyes for a moment, savoring the contact, even as she guessed that he was straining to keep things light between them, too.

"Thank you. I'm so hungry, I might not notice if I was chewing on a rawhide bone." She lifted her glass to toast the chef. "Cheers to you."

He clinked his chilled water to hers. "I'd rather drink to a night I'll never forget."

Surprise nearly made her slosh her beverage over the side. She wasn't prepared to talk about what had just happened between them when she hadn't had enough time to pick through the events in her mind. To resurrect those defenses she needed so desperately.

"Cheers," she said gamely, not wanting to draw even more attention to her post-wedding-night awkwardness. She gulped the water too fast and then dug in to her meal.

Gabe didn't call her on her gracelessness, letting the moment slip past without comment. When she'd sated the worst of her hunger, she searched for a topic to move them back to safer conversational ground, and distract her from how good he looked shirtless.

"Did you let your grandfather know that you've arrived?" As she buttered a slice of crusty warm bread, she realized she'd never complimented him on the meal. "The food is delicious, by the way. I'm so busy scarfing it down I didn't say as much, but thank you."

"My pleasure." Gabe ate more slowly than her, leaning back in the padded leather bar stool to watch her. "I sent a message to my grandfather when our plane landed. I notified my half brother Quinn, who is staying with him, as well."

She frowned. "Wasn't it Ian who was staying with Malcolm? Ian was the one who called you and let you know your grandfather was staying on in Cheyenne."

"True." Gabe picked up the bottle of red wine that they'd shared in the hot tub. He must have gone outside to retrieve it. He poured them each a glass. "But Ian and his wife were expected in Singapore this week, where the family is involved in a remodel of a flagship McNeill property. Lydia, Ian's wife, is an interior decorator."

The apartment where her grandmother was ensconced belonged to Ian and Lydia, Brianne recalled. It made sense Lydia was a decorator, given how beautiful that space was.

"Ian and Quinn tag-teamed staying with Malcolm?" Spearing a little more salad, she wished she'd had better relationships with her half siblings. It would have been nice to know someone she trusted was watching over Nana when Brianne wasn't with her.

A gust of wind beat against the windowpanes.

"Correct. Cameron helps out as well. From what I can see, Liam's other sons are all very close to Malcolm. Much closer to the old man than to our father, Liam." Frowning, Gabe took a sip of wine as if to wash away the taste of his father's name. "But that's something I've come to admire about them. Even though Quinn, Ian and Cameron are legally recognized as Liam's sons, they don't show Liam any more allegiance than Damon, Jager and I do."

Liam wasn't all that different from her own father.

She wondered if Liam's older brother was a higher quality character. Plus, talking about Gabe's family meant delaying discussion of where things were headed for them in this new marriage, which was a conversation she still wasn't ready to have.

"What about Donovan, Malcolm's estranged son?" She pushed her plate aside and leaned back in her chair. "Do you know much about him or what kind of person he is?"

"My grandfather never mentioned him when I met Malcolm briefly last fall." Gabe finished his wine and started to clear their plates. "I'm hoping to learn more about Donovan when we visit my grandfather tomorrow for dinner."

"We?" Brianne hopped up to help even though he tried to wave her off. She rinsed the dishes while he cleaned the countertops. They'd always made a good team when it came to working together.

"Malcolm is anxious, of course, to meet my wife. He told me as much on the phone." He moved around her as she stood at the sink, his body brushing hers in a way that made her nerve endings sing.

He dropped a kiss on her shoulder when he added a plate to her pile of dishes.

"Of course." With an effort, she focused on her words and not the contact that made her want to sway toward him. "Securing Malcolm's favor is the main reason we married."

She said it more as a reminder to herself, a piece of reality she couldn't ignore in her growing romantic feelings for Gabe.

But the effect on Gabe was tangible. He went still. For a moment, the only sounds in the kitchen were the ticking of a heavy wall clock and the howl of the wind.

"Gabe?" Turning toward him, she shook the water from her hands and dried them. "What's wrong?"

He stared down at his phone screen as he stood motionless at the island.

"There's something I didn't tell you about the wedding." His jaw flexed as he met her gaze. "About my other reason for needing a wife."

She didn't miss his word choice.

A wife. Not necessarily Brianne. Just a woman filling the role of legal spouse. A chill came over her, but she resisted the urge to wrap her arms around herself. She wouldn't show weakness now when she was already so vulnerable.

"What reason?" She willed strength into her voice even as it leaked out of her limbs.

He passed her the phone. She glanced down at the screen to see one of the wedding photos. Gabe was holding Jason in his arms and Brianne was clutching her delphiniums and wearing that gorgeous lace dress. At first, she didn't understand what the photo had to do with anything. But then, she spied the caption.

Country music queen Theresa Bauder's ex-husband, Gabe McNeill, takes his revenge on the singer with a quickie marriage to the former couple's gardener.

The photo was part of a tabloid story on some on-line gossip site. It was the private photo taken by a trusted employee of Ian McNeill.

Passing back the phone without reading the rest of the article, Brianne shook her head.

"I don't understand." She battled the sick feeling in her stomach from being made to look like an afterthought in Gabe's life. A woman not worthy of being named. "What does this have to do with your other reason for marrying me?"

When he drew in a breath, giving her a second to shift the puzzle pieces around in her mind, she suddenly understood perfectly.

"Oh, my God." Her knees didn't feel quite steady under her. She reached for the granite counter reflexively. "This is what you intended all along. I'm nothing more than revenge on your ex-wife."

Regret stung Gabe hard. He'd mishandled things with Brianne, no question. He could see that now. He hadn't intended to hurt her, and yet he'd put her in the most awkward position imaginable with the media. The caption made her sound like she'd been domestic help for Theresa, when Brianne had been employed solely by his company.

Worse, he was responsible for that devastated expression on her face right now. And the dawning sense of betrayal in her eyes.

"No." Shaking his head, he needed to explain himself. Fast. "I didn't marry you for any kind of revenge. Far from it."

But his new wife was already pacing the kitchen, anger and distrust evident in the quick churning of her feet, the impatient sweep of hair from her eyes.

"Yet this photograph was taken by a maid personally employed by your half brother's outrageously wealthy wife. Am I to believe she sold out the Mc-Neills for the sake of a few hundred bucks from a tabloid?" She shook her head. "The McNeills are notoriously private and they pay their servants well to protect their interests."

"Please, Brianne." He set aside the phone and took a step after her. "Listen."

"I should know, right?" She swung around to face him, holding her hands above her head in disbelief. "As one of your employees—your *gardener*— I signed confidentiality agreements, too."

He needed to end this line of argument before she got any more wound up. It was time to set the record straight. "I compensated the maid to distribute the photo to the press."

Brianne's mouth dropped open for a moment before she snapped it shut again. "Without mentioning it to me. Why would you do that if not to get under Theresa's skin?"

"I wanted the nuptials to be a matter of public record as quickly as possible." He ground his teeth. He wasn't accustomed to justifying himself or his actions to anyone.

But in a marriage, he understood he needed to make a better effort at that. When he and Theresa had been together, their lives had run on parallel tracks; they hadn't really connected. If he wanted a better relationship with Brianne, he would have to work on communication.

And, damn it, he did want a better relationship. He'd thought they were already on their way to having one.

"It's a legal union and very much part of the public record even without paparazzi coverage," she reminded him, folding her arms across her chest.

In her spa robe with tousled dark hair spilling down her shoulders, she looked more vulnerable than in her day-to-day cargo pants and T-shirts with her hair scraped back in a ponytail. He doubly regretted not discussing this before their wedding night. He couldn't stand the thought of her believing the worst about him after the incredible things they'd just shared.

"What I meant to say is that I wanted to make Theresa's publicity team and attorneys aware of our connection as soon as possible and I knew this would be the fastest approach." He ventured another step closer. "Can we sit down to talk about this?"

"I'm not sure what there is to discuss." Brianne didn't budge. She simply stared at him from the far end of the formal dining table for twelve cut from a raw hardwood slab. "You used our privately contracted union as a way to get on your ex-wife's radar. Either you want her attention, or you want to make her regret her loss. I can't imagine any other reason you'd do this, especially when you purposely didn't mention the plan to the bride."

Right. The only positive about the situation was that the more Brianne talked, the more Gabe understood why his actions hurt her to this degree. Of course, understanding didn't do anything to erase what he'd done. But seeing the way this affected her—knowing that he'd upset her this much—pained him. When he'd hidden the full intent of his agenda, he never guessed she'd view his omission in this light.

"I can see now why you might think that." He took another step closer, hoping he could salvage this night. He wanted to touch her. Hold her. "But I only used the leak as a way to fast-track the news so that everyone in Theresa's camp knows that Jason is in a stable, two-parent home."

Brianne pursed her lips and tilted her head to one side. "I don't understand why that's relevant. You've assured me, numerous times, that you want to encourage Jason's mom to be a part of his life."

"I do." He wished, more than anything, that his son would know the unconditional love of both his parents. "But despite my best efforts to facilitate visits between Jason and Theresa, she has resisted every overture." He'd never been comfortable sharing the deepest disappointments of his life, but he'd have to offer Brianne a whole lot more than he had before. "Until last week, when she phoned to say she wanted to get together with Jason for a Valentine's Day photo shoot an online feature about her new album."

Brianne frowned. "She doesn't visit for Jason's

sake, but when she needs an adorable baby in her pictures she's ready for a meeting?"

Gabe hated the way that made Theresa sound. But he'd certainly thought as much himself. Truth just stunk sometimes. Especially when it came to his ex.

"I'm hoping that this is a product of immaturity and being excited about all the new career opportunities." He had to hope for the best. "But if she's truly not going to be a meaningful part of his life, I can't afford to have her show up whenever she wants to jet our son around the globe because he's a useful accessory for her public image."

Brianne let out a low whistle between her teeth. "And you think that letting her know about our marriage will make her less likely to do that?"

"Not in the slightest. But if she ever gets the idea to sue for custody and renegotiate the terms we've agreed to, I think her attorneys will tell her she doesn't have a shot of winning Jason back permanently." Gabe needed to protect his son at all costs. And if Theresa refused to put the boy's best interests first, Gabe would be Jason's advocate and protector. "I want the people around her to know what they'd be up against before they try coming after the child Theresa abandoned."

Finally, Brianne nodded. Her arms fell back to her sides even if her expression was still guarded. "I can understand that, Gabe. You want to protect Jason's best interests, and that's honorable. But I wish you'd just let me know your plan to disseminate our wedding photo to the media."

He reached for her, wrapping a hand around her wrist beneath the heavy robe sleeve. "I'm still coming to terms with how I failed Jason when I couldn't make Theresa stay." He rubbed his thumb along the soft skin on the inside of her wrist. "It hurts to admit to myself, let alone share it with you. But I should have."

Slowly, she nodded. "And that's your biggest reason for entering this union to start with, isn't it? It wasn't so much about Malcolm's will as making sure Jason was safe?"

"I can guarantee Jason has an inheritance no matter what Malcolm decides." Gabe would work his ass off his whole life to ensure Jason had security. "But I can't protect my son if a judge decides Theresa deserves another chance to abandon him. Or to break the boy's heart when he's old enough to be hurt by her inconsistency."

Brianne nibbled her lip, her gaze shifting away from him to stare out the floor-to-ceiling windows at the spinning snow squall blowing at the glass.

"And what about a year from now, when our contracted time together ends?" she asked finally, her voice a barely there scrape of sound as she returned her gaze to his. "How will you protect him then?"

Gabe had already been thinking about that, of course. Not that he'd planned on sharing the idea with her. But he'd just learned that keeping his agenda private wasn't a good way to proceed with Brianne. Perhaps he'd be better served confiding the possibility that had been teasing the corner of his mind ever since he got the idea for the marriage.

Gently, he swept her hair behind her shoulder, smoothing his hand over the dark waves still a little curly from their dip in the hot tub.

"That agreement we signed is just to be sure you have everything you need if we sever our union." He'd read it carefully. Double-checked the wording. "There's nothing in there that says we *ever* have to end this marriage."

Eleven

Stay married?

The next day, the shock from Gabe's proposition still circled around in Brianne's mind as she sat alone in the master suite, the clear, bright Wyoming sun streaking in through the windows lining one wall.

She had been too exhausted and stunned the night before to press him about what he meant. She'd avoided responding altogether, redirecting the conversation toward their next meal. And then after her late dinner, she went to sleep. Or pretended to sleep.

Between the travel, the worries about her grandmother and all the directions Brianne's emotions had been tugged in, she simply didn't have the resources to quiz Gabe about his radical implication that they could remain married.

He'd probably been as tired as her and not thinking clearly anyhow. She'd pleaded for a time-out on
the discussion and hoped that things would make
more sense in the light of a new day. Her mind in
turmoil, she'd finally fallen asleep in Gabe's arms
and barely moved this morning when he told her he
was going to make some preparations for the meeting with Malcolm and Quinn today.

Now, three hours later, he still hadn't returned,
but he'd texted her that she should dress casually for
dinner tonight since they were taking a snowmobile
over to the main ranch house.

A snowmobile.

She was kind of excited about that, even though
she worried that casual attire wouldn't be right for
meeting Gabe's superwealthy grandfather, who probably traveled with a whole fleet of servants. Not to
mention the McNeill cousins that Malcolm had so
far won over in his efforts to connect with Donovan's family. Brianne decided to dress in her nicest
jeans and a butter-colored cashmere sweater she'd
discovered in the closet. Gabe had requested plenty
of wardrobe choices for her, his thoughtfulness all
the more welcome since she didn't own a winter
wardrobe.

But even hours after she'd rolled out of bed, she
was just as confused as ever about her conversation
with Gabe last night. Would he really sacrifice his
chance at true love to give his son stability? Or had
he been implying that he could envision his feelings
for her growing into something more?

Butterflies flitted through her stomach at the thought of him falling for her. How many times had she secretly dreamed about him?

But she didn't dare to let herself hope. Not when there was a chance he might be thinking of a purely practical arrangement. Already she knew that sleeping with him had been a mistake, sure to hurt her in the long run. He hadn't been honest with her about his reasons for marrying her in the first place, quietly using their wedding photo to solidify his custody arrangement without letting her know. What else might he be keeping from her?

Desperate to divert her thoughts while she waited for Gabe to return, Brianne curled into one of the matching recliners in the master suite and opened her laptop to check the photos emailed by the security company that had packed up Nana's apartment. There were so many images, including a video of the entire operation, but she could easily sort through the items by room, including the findings in the broom closet.

Not that she deluded herself Nana had hidden away anything terribly valuable. But she was curious to know what her grandmother had deemed most important to keep out of Wendy's hands. After fast-forwarding the video through to the broom closet and the removal of the very clever false wall, Brianne set the video footage at regular speed and watched.

The guys in charge of the packing were systematic, holding up item after item for the camera and cataloging what went into their boxes. Sometimes they narrated what they were doing, sometimes not, but everything was numbered and itemized.

"Autographed copy of the Beatles' *A Hard Day's Night*," the first packer said in a monotone for the camera.

"Autographed?" the other packer asked, his hand reaching forward into the picture. "By who?"

"It says it's 'To Rose.' Looks like all the Beatles signed it." Packer Number One—a muscular man in a tight-fitted T-shirt only visible from the back—pointed to the writing on the record sleeve. "Here's John Lennon's signature. And the other three are here."

Brianne couldn't believe her ears.

He passed the record into a box, while, off camera, the other packer let out a string of soft curses. "Are you kidding?"

She hit the pause button on the video, thinking. Brianne knew that her grandmother had met a lot of famous people during the years she'd worked as a singer. But the Beatles? And were records like that worth anything if they weren't in great condition? Nana's treasures had been packed away for a long time.

When she tuned back into the video, the guys were hauling out a lot more music memorabilia from Rose Hanson's brief career. She'd married her piano player, but the union had been tumultuous and Nana had kicked her cheating husband to the curb within a year; they'd been married just long enough for her to give birth to Brianne's father. And, of course, that cut short her time on stage.

Now those years of Nana's life were returning in full color as the two strangers pulled treasure after treasure out of that broom closet. There were what appeared to be mint-condition posters from performances Rose had given that had been headlined by groups like the Platters and Bill Haley and the Comets. Other posters advertised Rose as the main act and featured photos of her that Brianne had never seen. One showed Rose dancing on stage while shaking maracas, dressed in a gorgeous costume. Rose had given up everything she'd worked for to raise a son who hadn't been good to her. Brianne had her own reasons for resenting her father, but now she saw his selfishness through fresh eyes. And it made her more determined than ever to be true to herself.

True to her heart and her own dreams.

Brianne wasn't certain how much time had passed when Gabe appeared in the master suite. But seeing him in the doorway, his arms full of shopping bags, made her realize that the sun had almost set. Out the windows, twilight cast purple shadows in the room.

"Is everything all right?" Gabe set down the purchases on the floor, then crossed the room to join her, his blue eyes unswerving from her face.

He was undeniably handsome. He had a few snowflakes in his dark hair, and his coat and scarf were open, revealing a jacket and tie with dark jeans—his answer to Cheyenne casual, apparently.

"I'm fine." Self-conscious, Brianne swiped at a

tear that she hadn't realized was trickling down her cheek. "I'm just looking over the memorabilia from Nana's music career that she had hidden away."

"Music career?" Gabe frowned, and it wasn't until that moment that Brianne made the connection between Rose and Gabe's first wife, Theresa.

And the very different choice Nana had made as a mother. Then again, maybe that was simply a product of the times. If she had it to do all over again, would Nana still leave her singing career to be a full-time mother?

One thing was certain: if she'd chosen to keep singing, she would have found a way to balance motherhood and work. Abandoning an innocent child would have never occurred to Nana.

"Yes." Brianne turned the laptop around so he could see the still images she'd been reviewing— all the concert posters, photos of Nana with famous people, signed records and matchbook covers. There were a few costumes and pairs of shoes. "Nana gave up her career when she married and had my father, but she kept some of the things from her days as a singer."

Just like Gabe was giving up everything for his son. The work that he liked best. The chance at real love to be with a woman he trusted to care for Jason. Suddenly, his proposal that they stay married made more sense. And yes, Brianne had been foolish to think for a minute he could be falling for her.

Cold from the outdoors still hovered on Gabe's coat. It didn't keep her from wanting to get closer to him. Memories of the night before had been blind-siding her all day long. Vivid, sensual thoughts about the way he had made her feel kept twisting up with the sense of betrayal that had come afterward. The frustration of knowing he would hold on to their marriage for the sake of his child. She understood, but it still hurt to be used that way.

"Wow." Gabe used the touch screen to scan through the photos and pull up one of Nana on stage. "I can sure see the resemblance to you in this."

"Really?" Brianne tipped her head to see the screen better, more than willing to be distracted from the painful direction of her thoughts. "Do you think so?"

"For sure." He sketched a touch along the screen. "Through the eyes and mouth. A great beauty, just like her granddaughter." Turning Brianne's chin toward him, he kissed her lips.

Slowly. Thoroughly.

Her laptop would have fallen if he didn't catch it when it started sliding. Setting it aside, Gabe pressed closer. She lost herself in the kiss. The touches. Gabe had been the man she dreamed about for so long, and the reality of his arms around her was so much better than she'd ever imagined.

And maybe a part of her needed this moment with him to reassure herself last night hadn't been a fluke. That the chemistry between them was every bit as amazing as she'd thought.

"Put your arms around me." Gabe's whispered command told her he wanted the same thing she did.

Wordlessly, she gripped him, her defenses melting away like they'd never existed.

"Hold on tight," he told her, right before he lifted her from the chair.

And deposited her on the nearby bed.

The need for him was a physical ache this time. She pulled impatiently at her own clothes while he shed his. His efforts were more effective, however, his hands steadier as he ditched his shirt, pants and everything else. Her fingers were shaky from how much she wanted this. Him.

When he joined her on the bed, he made quick work of the rest of her clothes, kissing her all the while. Closing her eyes, she allowed herself to simply feel.

He lingered over her breasts, igniting an answering heat between her thighs. She clutched his shoulders harder, needing the completion he could bring. Restless and hungry for more, she arched into him. His groan was gratifying, a rough acknowledgment of how much he wanted her, too. By the time he entered her, she was beyond ready for him. The feeling transported her, taking her higher with every movement of his hips. Every skilled kiss.

She tossed her head against the pillow, seeking the bliss he had shown her the night before, a surprise gift that she hoped to feel again.

"Brianne." Her name on his lips was as tempting as his touches, especially when his eyes locked on hers.

She wanted to lose herself in this feeling. To stay

here with him until they understood one another. Until this heat between them made sense and she could give him everything. Not just her body, but her heart.

The realization rolled through her at the same moment Gabe shifted the pace, thrusting harder.

The tension inside her went taut for an instant. Then her release came, hard, fast spasms that made her shudder over and over. Maybe it was the way she moved against Gabe that made him find his own peak right afterward. Their shouts mingled, leaving her breathless and spent.

Leaving her certain she'd never experienced a more perfect moment. Though as he shifted to lie beside her, she had to acknowledge that it would have been even more perfect if Gabe trusted her enough to be honest with her.

If he loved her the way she'd loved him.

Wrenching her eyes open, she knew it was futile to deny it. Her heart had been Gabe's since long before this marriage. But now he possessed the power to hurt her more deeply. How unwise how she would be to allow that to happen again and muddle her thoughts.

"We should head over to your grandfather's." She untwined her legs from his and levered up on one elbow, her body still humming pleasantly from Gabe's lovemaking. Except it couldn't really be lovemaking, could it? Not when Gabe didn't return her feelings.

"What's wrong?" He studied her face, no doubt sensing her retreat. His hand covered her hip.

Even now, with her emotions raw and her body sated, she felt herself sway toward him.

Wanting him again.

"This is all happening too fast for me." That was true enough even though there were more complicated reasons for why she wanted to keep her distance. She needed to be true to herself and follow her dreams instead of swooning over a man who would never love her. "I will execute our agreement, Gabe, but I think we'd be wise to keep physical intimacy out of the arrangement."

Gabe gave the throttle more gas, pushing the snowmobile faster as he sped the few miles between the guest cabin and the main ranch house.

Riding behind Gabe, Brianne wrapped her arms around his waist and tucked her head against his back, her warmth welcome even though he knew the contact wouldn't be happening if not for the excuse of the snowmobile ride.

He'd screwed up with her and didn't know how to fix it. His heart wasn't in this meeting with Malcolm, but maybe spending the evening with outsiders would give Gabe a better handle on how to approach Brianne.

Clearly she hadn't forgiven him for not being more forthright about his reasons for marriage. And he understood. But didn't their connection override that? He'd thought, after she'd let her guard down with him again, that she was willing to move forward, but that hadn't been the case. He'd been stunned when she'd pulled away after sex.

He regretted hurting her. More than he could say. But at least he'd been honest about taking a more mercenary approach to matrimony.

Who wouldn't after what he'd gone through with Theresa?

Snow swirled in his face as he turned the sled down a well-marked path. The terrain was firmer here, the snow hard-packed, and the machine picked up speed. He could feel Brianne tip her head back, experimentally extending a hand into the rooster tail of snow that kicked up as he turned.

"Careful," he warned, needing to keep her safe.

"It's so beautiful out here," she shouted over the roar of the motor as her hand slid around his waist again.

He ground his teeth together against the seductive feel of her touch. A touch she wouldn't be sharing with him anytime soon unless he could figure out a way to fix things between them.

He had bought early Valentine's Day gifts for her this afternoon, hoping to entice her to stay in Cheyenne for the next week. After seeing the acres of pristine forests for himself, he wanted to share it with his son. He'd made arrangements for Nadine and Jason to travel tomorrow so they could all be together in this winter wonderland.

But it wouldn't be as fun if Brianne didn't want to be a part of it.

As the main ranch house came into sight, lights

blazing in every window of the three-story Craftsman facade, Gabe slowed the snowmobile. Similar in style and construction to the guest cottage where he and Brianne were staying, the main house was bigger with more rooflines and additions. For a moment, Gabe felt the itch to run a hand over the rough, unfinished beams providing support to the building, his carpenter's eye seeing more possibilities in the wood.

But he wasn't a carpenter anymore, he reminded himself as he helped Brianne off the seat. For his son's sake, he was going to form a relationship with Malcolm McNeill and become a part of the man's formidable empire. He ground his teeth, remembering Brianne's words to him just a few days ago.

What if you teach your son that success can be found in things that make you happy?

She had a point, of course. But for now, success came in the form of McNeill Resorts. Until Jason had a stake in the company, the one that he was legally entitled to as an heir, Gabe's personal pursuits would have to wait.

Beside him, Brianne tugged off her shiny metallic helmet and set it on the seat of the snowmobile.

"I hope you let me drive home." She combed her fingers through the dark hair she'd swept into a high ponytail. She was flustered and he knew that had to do with the awareness between them. "That looked like fun."

He knew she was confused about their relationship and he regretted that.

"There's not much I wouldn't give to make you

happy, Brianne." He wondered if she had any idea how important she'd become to him.

Not just since the wedding, either.

He was beginning to see that she was one of the most honest voices in his life, and her opinions were something he could count on. That had been true since long before the wedding vows.

Her smile faltered for a moment before she recovered. She was putting a wall up between them, so thin he could see right through. "If you mean it, then please don't let me make a fool of myself in front of your family tonight."

At first, he found it hard to believe she was serious. But then he recalled the insecurity her stepmother had instilled in her at a young age.

"They'll be fortunate to know you." He wanted to fold her in his arms. Kiss her until she bloomed with self-confidence and sensual fulfillment. But he would honor her request about physical intimacy until he could—he hoped—change her mind. "Come on."

He took her hand and led her toward the front door. He'd touched her that way when they were just friends, so he wasn't going to stop now.

"I did some reading on Quinn." Her breath formed a visible cloud in the cold air. "He has his own hedge fund. I think that makes him wealthy enough to buy and sell small countries."

Gabe paused in front of the wide steps leading to the front door. "Someone once told me that success isn't about making a buck. Remember?"

She worried her lower lip, her uncertainty visible in her eyes as they stood under the bright porch lights. "Does anyone in the McNeill family believe that, though?"

"As long as you believe it, that's all that matters." He didn't like the idea of Brianne being intimidated by anyone in his family. He was already regretting the way their wedding photo had circulated with the caption referring to her as his anonymous gardener.

Why hadn't they simply used her name? She was so much more than her job.

"I do believe that." Nodding, she tucked her free hand into the pocket of her red parka. "Thank you for the reminder."

They headed up the stairs toward the eight-foot-tall double doors with matching sidelights. The design was impressive but his carpenter eye couldn't help but reimagine the space. He rang the bell, then heard the latch turning and the right door swung wide.

"Welcome, brother." The tall guy who extended his hand had the look of the McNeills: the blue eyes, dark hair and same sharp jaw that Gabe saw in the mirror every day.

But even in a relaxed pair of chinos and a dark button-down shirt, Quinn was a shade more refined than the others. Certainly more so than Gabe, Damon and Jager. Quinn's hair looked like it saw a barber often, for one thing. For another, Gabe could spot the difference between his own custom-made shirts and the kind of threads Quinn sported. The personal tailoring took high-end to the next level.

"Brianne, this is my oldest brother, Quinn. Quinn, I'd like you to meet my new wife, Brianne McNeill. Formerly Hanson." He presented her quickly, hoping she wouldn't be nervous.

Her grin looked relaxed enough now. "Nice to meet you, Quinn. And excuse me for gawking, but the family resemblance is uncanny."

If anyone was gawking, it was Gabe. At her. She was so beautiful. So charming and unpretentious with her warm smile. His chest ached at the thought of disappointing her somehow. He's been her husband for a day and he was already screwing up his marriage.

Quinn smiled warmly at her as he took their coats and hung them in a nearby closet. "I understand completely since I still do a double take when I see Cameron with Damon. Welcome to the rapidly expanding McNeill family. Come on in. Gramps can't wait to meet you."

Gabe took in the relaxed decor of the ranch house. The rooms were sprawling and emphasized space over furnishings, although perhaps that was because the place had been on the market.

"Rapidly expanding?" Brianne seized on Quinn's words as they strode deeper into the house, past a main-floor guest room, formal dining room and a bar area, every room well lit.

The scent of a meal hung in the air. There were savory spices and a lemony sweetness, too.

"Sorry." Quinn paused by a series of cowboy paintings in the wide corridor. "I didn't mean that to be as crass as it sounded. I've just been going a few rounds with Gramps, trying to ascertain the full extent of the family history before he springs any more relatives on us."

"You can't blame Malcolm for my brothers and me," Gabe reminded him. He'd come to terms with the fact that he had a useless father years ago, so he was hardly going to apologize for it. Quinn surely knew how it felt to have the man check out on him. "That was all Liam's doing."

"And from what we both know of our father's global adventures, I wouldn't be surprised if he reveals other offspring one day." Quinn shrugged before he continued down the hall. "My frustration today is that Malcolm erased all traces of his older son from our world—no photos, no shared memories, no nothing. And then, twenty-seven years after his feud with the guy, he wants a reunion even though our uncle is clearly still hostile about the split."

"That's a long time to hold a grudge," Brianne said, lowering her voice as they stepped down into a sunken family room with leather couches and a huge, two-sided stone fireplace.

Gabe spotted his grandfather already seated in a chair-and-a-half, a highball glass and folded copy of a New York newspaper on the cocktail table beside him.

"Gramps, our guests are here," Quinn called into the room.

Automatically, Gabe slid an arm around Brianne's waist. Was it a protective instinct? Or simply a chance to touch her when he craved being close
to her? He breathed deep, hoping for a hint of her
fragrance.

"It's a good thing." Malcolm lifted a mahogany
cane in a kind of salute toward them, but did not get
to his feet. Silver-haired and blue-eyed, he wore an
honest-to-God smoking jacket over his suit. The red-
and-gold satin coat was belted at the waist. "Some
of my grandsons are getting weary of my company,
it seems. I need new relatives to bother."

Gabe drew Brianne over to his grandfather's
chair while Quinn followed behind them and said,
"Gramps, you're not a bother."

Malcolm winked at Gabe and extended his hand.
"It's an old man's prerogative to be a pest to his family. Good to meet you, Gabe. It means a lot that you
traveled all this way to see me."

Gabe ignored the extended hand and went in for
the hug, giving his grandfather a squeeze around
his shoulders. "Truth be told, I was glad to learn my
father had quality people in his family. It gave me
some hope for me." He was only partly joking. He
turned to Brianne. "Granddad, this is my wife, Brianne Hanson McNeill."

"Brianne." Malcolm enveloped Brianne's hand
in both of his. "Welcome to the family, my dear."

"Thank you, sir." She leaned closer and kissed
the man's cheek. "I don't have much family of my
own. I've been looking forward to meeting Gabe's."

Malcolm fairly cackled at that. "You see, Quinn?" He turned in his chair toward his other grandson. "Not everyone is getting tired of having relatives."

"I like relatives just fine, Gramps. It's secrets that I'm not so crazy about." Quinn lifted his drink in a silent toast behind his grandfather's head. "Gabe, there's a wet bar against the far wall if you or Brianne would like a drink. I'm going to check on dinner."

Excusing himself, Quinn stepped away, leaving Gabe alone with Brianne and Malcolm.

"Brianne, can I get you anything?" Gabe moved toward a granite-topped cart with a handful of decanted drinks.

"Club soda or water would be great." She took the seat closest to his grandfather, setting her beaded yellow clutch on the hearth nearby.

While Gabe poured two drinks, he heard Malcolm settling back in his chair.

"So how was your trip, my dear?" Malcolm asked her. "I know it was difficult to coordinate flights from opposite coasts."

Brianne paused a moment, as did Gabe. He glanced over his shoulder toward his grandfather, wondering if the older man's health issues led to confusion sometimes.

"Gabe and I flew together from New York, actually." Brianne answered after a beat. "We thought a trip to Wyoming sounded like a fun honeymoon."

A drink in each hand, Gabe moved to rejoin them. Malcolm laughed as he retrieved his drink from the cocktail table. "A belated honeymoon, considering you have a son. How old is the boy again?"

"Grandad, you must be confusing Brianne with my former wife." Gabe passed her a glass and settled into the leather love seat next to her. "Brianne and I just got married yesterday."

Frowning, Malcolm picked at the belt on his smoking jacket. "You're not the singer?" he asked finally, peering up at Brianne. "Flying in from LA?"

Gabe tensed, knowing his ex-wife was the last topic Brianne would wish to discuss, especially given their disagreement the night before.

"I'm a landscape designer," Brianne said politely to clarify, though Gabe could see the stiff set to her shoulders. "Gabe's ex-wife is a singer."

Malcolm's frown deepened.

"I fear I have been talking to the wrong person online." Malcolm reached over to the cocktail table by his chair, knocking his newspaper off as he patted around for his cell phone. Turning on the screen, he thumbed through applications. "I got a direct message on Twitter after I announced a visit from Gabe and his wife."

A knot fisted in Gabe's chest. Rising, he went to the older man's side. Gabe glanced over at Brianne, but she stared into the flames snapping and popping in the huge fireplace. Her jaw was set.

"Here it is." Malcolm held up the phone so Gabe could see. "Theresa someone?"

"Bauder." Gabe tilted the screen so he could read

without a glare. See you soon, Gramps. Where are you staying this week?

Brianne's head whipped around. "Does she have this address?"

Malcolm shook his head. "I'm so sorry, Brianne. I thought I was talking to—"

"Gabe's wife," she said, finishing for him, her polite smile tight. "It's an understandable mistake."

Anger simmered that Gabe's ex-wife would pull a stunt like this. He thumbed through the exchange, which included directions to the Cheyenne ranch, small talk about Jason—which was rich considering she hadn't seen her son in months—and an assurance she would arrive "soon" for a visit.

"But I would have never invited her if I had realized..." Malcolm trailed off, clearly flustered. "Maybe Quinn will have an idea how we can fix this. Or I could message her—"

"No need." Brianne rose from her seat and laid a comforting hand on his arm. "Please don't worry on my account. It's fine. And considering how little notice Theresa had about this marriage, I don't blame her for the confusion, either." She lifted her dark gaze to Gabe. "I think a family meeting is overdue."

Twelve

Every time the doorbell rang at the ranch house, Brianne held her breath, convinced that Gabe's ex-wife would come waltzing into the living room with her music-industry entourage and couture clothes. Although Brianne had never had much direct interaction with the woman when Theresa had resided at the Birdsong, Brianne sure remembered the emotional wreckage after her defection. Gabe had poured everything into convincing her to return home. How would he feel to see her again? Of course, as protective as Brianne might be about him, those emotions were a double-edged sword since any pain Gabe might experience could also indicate his feelings for Theresa still lingered.

By comparison, meeting Gabe's Wyoming cousins tonight suddenly seemed far less intimidating.

During the cocktail hour before dinner, Brianne received an education on Donovan McNeill's offspring, half of whom had agreed to give their grandfather a chance and shown up at the evening gathering. At least trying to keep the McNeill relatives straight helped Brianne take her mind off Theresa Bauder's possible appearance—and what that might mean to Gabe.

Malcolm had chosen to rent out this particular ranch house because it sat between a handful of properties northwest of Cheyenne owned by Donovan McNeill's family members, making it easy for them to travel here. Donovan had three sons with his first wife, ranch heiress Kara Calderon. Their oldest two boys were twins, Cody and Carson. The youngest, Brock, was the only one of Donovan's sons slated to show up this evening, though he hadn't arrived yet.

When Donovan's first wife died just a few years after Brock was born, Donovan had married local bartender Page Samara, with whom he had three girls, Madeline, Maisie and Scarlett. Maisie had arrived first tonight—on horseback in the dark, which apparently wasn't as dangerous as it sounded if you knew the terrain as well as she did. Dressed in jeans and red leather boots, Maisie's white blouse and long, angora sweater vest had a Western vibe without being too kitschy. No more than twenty-five, Maisie sat in a corner of the living room drinking

Chivas with her grandfather and relating the story of an accident in the lambing pen—whatever that was.

Her dark hair was chin-length and blunt-cut, her blue eyes paler than those of the McNeill men Brianne had met so far. Maisie was beautiful, utterly self-possessed and had a dry sense of humor. So, with that being Brianne's first introduction to Gabe's cousins, she was unprepared for Scarlett, the youngest of the siblings, who breezed in wearing an ice-blue lace dress, white go-go boots and dark hair with bangs, curls and crystal barrettes.

"Greetings, family!" She hailed Brianne and Gabe from the doorway, waving both arms as she spotted them on the other side of the living room.

Quinn was still trying to take her coat—a shearling jacket as long as her dress—yet Scarlett didn't stand still long enough, and came rushing down into the sunken living room with her arms wide.

Luckily, Gabe set down his drink before she reached him so that when she flung her arms around him, he didn't spill anything.

"It's great to meet you!" she trilled before edging back to study him more closely. "A McNeill who doesn't wear boots. I love it." She hugged him again before turning her bright blue gaze to Brianne. "Hi." She smiled crookedly. "You're totally gorgeous, but not who I was expecting. Gramps said—"

"Looks like your ticket to Los Angeles didn't pan out," Maisie said from her spot on the couch, patting the seat next to her. "Sit by me and I'll catch you up to speed on how Granddad mixed up our cousin's wives."

"Oh." Scarlett managed to appear both sympathetic to Brianne and disappointed at the same time. "Awkward but forgivable." She bent to kiss Malcolm's cheek. "I can barely keep track of my siblings, so I give you credit for keeping as many people straight as you do, Gramps."

Quinn dropped onto the sofa beside Brianne while Gabe's new cousins drew him into conversation about his plans in Cheyenne.

"Are you sure you don't want to upgrade that club soda to something stronger?" Quinn asked Brianne with a knowing look in his blue eyes.

"Actually, considering the evening I'm having, I'd better not drink anything that might loosen my tongue." She sipped her drink, feeling utterly out of place in this room full of McNeills.

She wasn't really one of them. And right now, she felt foolish for even making an appearance here tonight. She already understood that Gabe didn't have the same kind of feelings for her that she had for him. Why torment herself more at a gathering that was for family?

Quinn lowered his voice further while the volume in the rest of the room increased. "For what it's worth, I can tell you that my grandfather is mortified about his mistake."

Nearby in the kitchen, Brianne heard one of the catering staff exclaim in French. How funny that the language made her feel nostalgic for Martinique. The

Caribbean island wasn't her native land, but it was more home than anywhere else, and right now she felt like an interloper in Wyoming. She wondered how long she would have to remain by Gabe's side before she could return to the Birdsong with Rose and finish her landscape design work there.

As much as it would hurt not to see Gabe for weeks or months on end while he worked with Malcolm, Brianne knew it would be for the best if they resumed their lives separately. They could honor a contract marriage without living in the same home. She didn't want to ruin their friendship, the bond they'd spent a year building, although part of her feared they already had.

"I certainly don't blame your grandfather," Brianne assured Quinn, grateful for his kindness on a day when she felt so deeply alone. "Gabe and I just wed yesterday. Most people wouldn't know about the marriage anyway."

"But he takes pride in the family and knowing as much about each new member as possible." Quinn watched his grandfather for a moment before turning his gaze back to Brianne. "When he first came up with this idea that he wanted to change his will and require his heirs to be married, my brothers and I argued with him for weeks about it. He never wavered for a moment, insisting he wanted more family."

Tempted to tell him that the marriage requirement only fostered fake relationships, Brianne bit her tongue. It wasn't her place, and it wasn't her family. Still, she could weigh in diplomatically, couldn't she?

"He might be glad to surround himself with more family for now, but what if the influx of McNeills results in a spike in divorces because they rushed to the altar?" Maybe she hadn't bitten her tongue as well as she'd planned.

Quinn didn't appear alarmed by the idea, however. "Time will tell. I worried about that, too, at first. But now? I wonder if he knows what he's doing after all."

The doorbell rang again. Brianne's heart stuttered. Would Theresa's arrival be the end of her own tentative relationship with Gabe?

Gabe's gaze landed on her, but she refused to meet it, afraid of how much it might reveal about her feelings for him.

Grinding her teeth, she moved closer to Scarlett in the hope of drafting her into conversation while Quinn got the door.

"Brianne." Gabe's voice in her ear set her nerves on edge. "I'm sorry about this. We can leave if you want."

She shook her head in silence, straining to hear some hint of an exchange at the front door.

"My grandfather will understand," Gabe continued, his hand a warm presence on her shoulder.

"No. Thank you." She couldn't help the bite in her tone. The tension in the room was sharp enough to hurt.

Maisie leaned forward in her seat. "That's not Brock at the door," she announced. "It's a woman."

Brianne's stomach dropped. Still, she appreciated the warning because a moment later Theresa Bauder strode into the room. All six feet of her, rail-thin and lovely. Brianne was tempted to glance at Gabe to gauge his reaction, but she was afraid of what she might see.

Old feelings. Deeper feelings than he had toward her.

"I hope I'm not too late for the McNeill reunion." Theresa seemed to strike a pose on the step above the sunken living room. She wore a head-to-toe red pantsuit, and her brown leather bucket purse contained a tiny white papillon dog with fluffy, butter-fly-shaped ears.

Behind her trailed two more tall and spindly companions—a wheat blonde and a glossy bru-nette—each dressed in what looked like the run-way's answer to Western wear. One had a leather vest complete with silver bolo tie, but she wore it with a plaid, floor-length skirt.

"Theresa, this is a family meal," Gabe informed her wearily.

For a moment, Brianne empathized. She under-stood his disappointment in a woman who had aban-doned their son for purely selfish pursuits. Truly, she did. But unleashing yesterday's wedding photo on-line hadn't done anything to ease a difficult situation with a woman he already knew to be immature. And for that reason, Brianne made no move to help him.

"But as Jason's mother, I will *always* be family, Gabriel," his ex reminded him, motioning her co-horts forward as she started down the steps toward the group congregated around the stone fireplace. "I'm so excited for our Valentine's Day mother-son photo shoot next week in New York to publicize my new album. Have you told Jason about it?"

Brianne could feel the tension and resentment radiating off Gabe from all the way across the room. And yes, she couldn't deny an empathetic ache for him.

"Jason might be a little young to understand the photo shoot," Gabe finally said. "But he will be there."

Scarlett leaned closer to Brianne, curls brushing against her shoulder, and whispered, "Don't worry. Watch me dive on the land mine."

"Theresa Bauder!" Scarlett exclaimed at full volume, hurrying over to fuss over the newcomer's clothes, friends and dog, thoroughly distracting and welcoming Theresa at the same time.

While Scarlett made a noisy production of finding an appropriate water dish for the papillon, Brianne took a deep breath and plotted how to get through the meal. She'd endured her stepmother for years as a kid, so she could definitely handle one pampered singer for the course of a dinner. Thankfully, just then the caterer called them to the table, moving the evening along. Apparently they weren't going to wait any longer for Brock, Maisie and Scarlett's half brother, who had planned to join them.

"You will sit near me." Malcolm's voice rumbled in Brianne's ear. He walked beside her, leaning lightly on Quinn as the group moved toward the formal dining room.

The antler chandeliers were on a low setting, and candles flickered down the length of the table decorated with pink roses in heart-shaped red bowls in a Valentine's Day theme. The place settings were white china, but each woven mat had a smattering of red rose petals. Simple but pretty.

"Thank you," she told Malcolm, "but I can hold my own. You should enjoy your meal."

"I will enjoy it most learning more about you." He steered her toward the chair at his right as they approached the table. "I insist."

"I'll take the flank," Maisie announced, grabbing the seat on Brianne's other side. The woman's dark hair fell forward as she tucked her chair into place. "Since husbands and wives can't sit together anyhow. Scarlett might provide good interference, but honey, I'm the *wall* when it comes to annoying women."

Maisie reached for the bottle of red wine on the table and poured herself a glass. Brianne couldn't resist a smile. She didn't believe in girl bashing on principle, but exceptions could be made for ex-wives who chose to stir trouble. It upset Brianne to think that Theresa's idea of visitation with her child was a photo shoot to promote an album. The defensiveness Brianne felt for the boy made her glad that Gabe was protecting his custodial rights. No child should be subjected to the whims of a parent who couldn't be bothered to make real time for them.

"Thank you." Brianne's gaze went to Gabe briefly.

He and Quinn were attempting to work out a seating arrangement for the rest of the table while Scarlett and Theresa were coaxing the dog—apparently named Roxy—to her travel bed in a corner of the dining room.

"I'm guessing she only bothered showing because Malcolm McNeill is...Malcolm McNeill." Maisie sipped her wine, peering over the assembly with a cool, assessing gaze. "Everyone sees dollar signs when his name is mentioned."

"You think so?" It provided a small comfort to Brianne to think Gabe's grandfather was more of a target than Gabe himself.

Because no matter how much she told herself she wasn't falling for Gabe, it was happening. And fast.

It hurt to imagine the mother of his child returning to the picture and wooing him away from Brianne, even though a better woman than her might root for that exact scenario. Ideally, Jason would then know the love of his mother.

"She abandons her kid two weeks after his birth but suddenly wants to be at a McNeill gathering in Nowhere, Wyoming?" Maisie's dark eyebrow lifted before she rolled her eyes. "Trust me, money motivated this visit. Uh-oh." She nudged Brianne's arm and pointed to the corner of the dining room. "Look."

Gabe had engaged Theresa in conversation, and it was turning animated. Her girl squad had their phones at the ready, pretending to be texting but more likely taking photos or video.

Brianne didn't want to be a part of the drama.

Nowhere in her contract with Gabe did it say she needed to be involved in a public standoff with his ex. Especially when their marriage was a facade put into place for very specific reasons.

To protect Jason. To help Nana.

It was Brianne's fault for seeing more in the relationship than that. But she didn't need to keep making the same mistakes with Gabe, perceiving more in his actions and attention than what was really there. Gabe didn't need to make a fool of her. She'd managed as much just fine on her own.

Not anymore.

"Excuse me," Brianne murmured to her table companions, who were already engrossed in the developing drama. "I really need to get home."

She wasn't sure that anyone even noticed her slip out the door.

Gabe could not abide his ex-wife insinuating herself at his grandfather's dinner table—after she'd been completely absent from their son's life since mere weeks after his birth—on a night he had planned to make special for Brianne. He wanted Brianne to consider making this marriage permanent. He knew he could make her happy if she gave him the chance.

But he sure as hell wasn't off to a good start if he allowed Theresa and her friends to simply bluster their way into a family meal. Now, as he tried to reason with her quietly, she raised her voice.

"Why would I leave?" She threw her hands up in

the air as if the answer was obvious. "I have every right to know my son's family. It's only fair that I know the people he spends his time with while I'm busy pursuing my own career."

"Our son is not here," he reminded her, aware of all the eyes on them. Especially Brianne's. He hadn't wanted to hurt her like this. "And you haven't shown any interest in Jason since he was born, rejecting every single attempt I've made to help you spend time with him. I think it's important he has some sense of family around him, especially since his mother has been absent from his life."

"News flash, Gabe, you should be introducing our son to Malcolm McNeill instead of our *gardener*. Jason should be here, benefiting from that connection." Theresa pointed a red talon at his chest.

Tension turned to anger. He could not allow her to disrespect a woman with a heart as kind and tender as Brianne's, a woman who had always put the needs of the people she loved ahead of her own. A woman he was falling in love with, he realized.

The knowledge of his feelings was a wake-up call, an alarm that sounded louder than any of the smoke-screen arguments that Theresa made. Love for Brianne suddenly made everything else go quiet inside him. His feelings for her had been growing deeper every day for a year. The emotions had sneaked up on him because he'd seen it as friendship, and a father's appreciation for her kindness and warmth toward his child.

But it was so much more than that. He loved Brianne with a fierceness that wasn't going to go away in a year or an eternity.

"Brianne is my *wife*." The word meant everything to him. It had never meant much to Theresa, he knew, but Brianne devoted more to a fake marriage than Theresa had ever committed to a real one.

That alone spoke volumes about their respective characters. And, sadly, it said something about his that he'd given his heart to a woman who wasn't worthy of it, while he'd given a legal document to another who deserved the world at her feet.

"She is a domestic who stole you out from under me!" Theresa's voice hit a screechy note, and the theatrics of the performance made him aware of her friends trying to capture the scene on their camera phones.

Turning on his heel, Gabe had no more to say to her, or time for her piece of performance art. But as he looked back at the dinner table full of relatives he'd only just met, he realized the one person he needed to see most wasn't there.

The woman he loved.

Heart sinking along with his hopes of salvaging his marriage, Gabe sprinted for the door without saying good-night.

Thirteen

Outside the ranch house, the snow was falling again. Near the front steps, Gabe saw the snowmobile still parked with two helmets sitting on top. So Brianne hadn't taken it back to the guest cottage. While he felt a moment's relief that she wasn't driving alone on unfamiliar back roads in the dark, he wondered where she'd gone. He withdrew his phone from his pocket to call her and noticed she had messaged him.

Your cousin Brock arrived for dinner just as I was leaving. He gave me a ride. Please take your time and work things out with your family. I'm going to pick up Nana and bring her back to Martinique with me.

Not if Gabe had anything to say about it. Pocketing his phone, he strapped on a helmet and fired up the snowmobile, determined to reach her in time to change her mind. What if she'd convinced Brock to take her all the way to the airport? But he couldn't text her back now that he was speeding through the dark void of ranch acreage with only the half-moon overhead for light to guide him.

Brianne had been right. He'd made a tactical error in releasing the wedding photo the way he had, unwittingly antagonizing Theresa when he needed her goodwill and cooperation. He'd thought the strategy would ensure he spoke to Theresa less, but his ex-wife had also been right about one thing tonight—she would always be a part of his family and he could not afford to alienate Jason's mother. The situation with her would always require careful handling in order to give Jason the best possible experience with his mother, without flipping his world around anymore than it already had been, and likely would be again, given her temperament.

Branches scraped Gabe's face as he pushed the snowmobile as fast as it would go. He didn't want to give Brianne enough time to pack and leave, but he knew any truck could speed through the terrain faster than his vehicle.

A few minutes later, though, he reached the guest cottage and found the lights still on. There was no movement outside, but through the huge floor-to-ceiling windows, he caught a glimpse of Brianne moving from room to room.

Relief coursed through him even though he knew

the tougher job lay ahead of him. How would he convince her to stay? To take a chance on him again when he hadn't valued her or her opinions enough the first time?

She brought a sense of peace to his life he'd never known before. Well, peace and passion. His chest ached at the thought of losing her.

After killing the engine, he rushed to the front door and charged up the main staircase to her bedroom—the guest suite where she'd put her things even though they'd shared his bed the night before. He couldn't bear for it to be the last time. Not after what they'd shared. Not after the way she'd captured his heart so completely. This wasn't some friends-with-benefits situation. And it wasn't a marriage of convenience for him—not anymore. This was the real deal, and he couldn't accept that he might lose her.

"Brianne." Gabe knocked lightly on the door frame even though the door wasn't shut. He was unwilling to invade her space when she had every right to be angry with him.

Her suite was smaller than the master bedroom, but similarly decorated. There was a simple white duvet on the king-sized bed. The natural wood furnishings had yellow and red accents. A painting of the Grand Tetons sat on the mantel among a handful of antler accessories. Brianne had her suitcase on the bed, with several items already folded inside.

"I messaged you," she said, moving quickly as she

brought a toiletry bag from the bathroom toward the suitcase. "I'm going back to New York to get Nana."

"I saw your text." He wanted to touch her. Intercept her. But he could see the tangle of emotions in her eyes and worried about doing the wrong thing at a time when he could not afford a misstep. "Can we talk first, because—"

"I'm flying commercial. There's a flight in two hours. I really need to be on it." She thunked the bag into her suitcase and headed back toward the closet. "A car will be here to pick me up in—" she checked her phone screen "—ten minutes."

That left him no time. He stalked closer. "Let me drive you instead. Or we can fly back to New York together in the morning."

"I think it's better I do this on my own." Her dark eyes flipped up to meet his. No hesitation. No doubts.

She sidled past him and kept packing, her gaze refocused on her work.

Fear of losing her touched off a new fire in him. "I know I made a mistake when I released that photo to the media. But seeing Theresa again only made me realize how much of an idiot I would be to lose you, Brianne."

"You don't need to say that. You're not losing me. We have a year on our contract, and I plan to honor that. I'll hold you to your end of the bargain, too. But we can't live under the same roof. Not when—" She hesitated. Bit her lip. "Not when the boundaries get all mixed up."

He saw an opening. A chink in her plan and a

flicker of hope for them. "So let's get rid of the boundaries. I love you, Brianne. I don't want any more walls between us."

He could tell by her expression that he'd caught her off guard. She hadn't expected him to fall in love with her, but he had. Her lips moved soundlessly for a moment, but then she shook her head. Straightened.

"Perhaps you do love me," she acknowledged. "But what you feel for me is friendship. A camaraderie and trust that's important to both of us and that we don't want to sacrifice for the sake of a contract marriage." She tossed a couple of shirts into the suitcase without folding them, leaving behind all the shopping bags full of winter clothes he'd bought for her. "But that's not enough for the long haul, Gabe."

"I love you." He said it again, all the more certain of it. And certain that she was wrong to tell him how he felt. "And that's not enough?"

"You haven't even had time to grieve for your first marriage. I don't want to be the rebound romance only to have my heart shattered in a million pieces two years from now." She stuffed her arms in the sleeves of the red parka and shoved her phone in her pocket.

He was offering her everything and she was rejecting him? The fear inside him grew colder. "That wouldn't happen. I can promise you that family means everything to me."

"I know." She swiped a hand across her eyes. "For Jason's sake, you're willing to construct the facade of a family. But he deserves the real thing."

"This *is* the real thing," he insisted, knowing that he'd just seen the difference with his own eyes back at his grandfather's house. "I have no illusions about my ex-wife, Brianne. She never cared about me or our son."

"And I do." She sounded so certain of herself. "I always will. But my grandmother sacrificed everything to remove me from a dysfunctional family. I won't dishonor that by sliding right back into another situation where I have to fight for scraps of affection." She pursed her lips. "I love you, too, Gabe, but I deserve more."

He was so stunned, he didn't even move to carry her suitcase for her as she headed toward the door. She couldn't possibly turn her back on him. On the promise they'd made to each other.

"Brianne. Wait," he called out, belatedly rushing after her to try again to convince her of the truth.

To convince her that he understood about real love, damn it.

But she was already gone. He saw the taillights of an SUV glowing red in the Wyoming darkness as she rode away, taking his heart with her.

The next morning, Brianne awoke to the sound of a Count Basie recording playing a few rooms away.

Blinking against the bright sun streaming in, it took her a moment to remember where she was. She'd traveled more this week than she had in the whole rest of her life combined. New York. Cheyenne. New York again.

Resisting the urge to burrow deeper under the high-thread-count sheets, Brianne forced her eyelids all the way open while "Kid from Red Bank" reminded her of her grandmother's love for big-band music. Because who else besides Nana would be playing Count Basie? Nadine and Jason were still in the apartment, but she'd never heard Jason's nanny blasting horns and trumpets. Rose had lived and breathed swing and big-band music, though.

The nostalgia for visiting Nana's apartment as a kid was a small bright spot on a day when Brianne's heart threatened to shatter in a million pieces if she moved too quickly. Gabe had given her almost everything she could have ever wanted last night, even saying he loved her.

But how could she believe that when he'd had his heart torn out by the worst possible marriage experience less than a year ago? According to Gabe, Theresa had served him divorce papers as soon as she found out she was pregnant. He'd refused to sign them until after Jason was born, meaning his divorce was less than a year old.

Who could get married so fast after something like that and have the relationship be anything meaningful? No. Gabe had married her for a very specific reason, and he'd chosen her because she was his best friend.

She'd honor that friendship if it killed her. And judging by the way her heart felt today, it very well might. But she wasn't going to allow her friend to be hurt again. Not by her or anyone else. She could do that much for him.

As for her?

Her heart was toast already. That was no one's fault but her own. She'd allowed herself to sleep with him when she'd had a mad crush on him for over a year. Of course, that would turn out to be a disaster of epic proportions.

Forcing herself out of bed as "Kid from Red Bank" shifted into "One O'Clock Jump," Brianne told herself she still had her family. Having Nana back in her life was more than she'd expected to have at this point, so she should be celebrating that instead of crying over Gabe. Or celebrating that she'd stood up for herself, refusing to settle for less than true love.

But it was better to focus on Nana, since the refusing-to-settle part didn't feel like a victory when it left her so thoroughly hollow inside.

She washed her face and brushed her teeth, then dressed slowly. It was late again—almost noon. Her schedule had been out of whack between the travel and the late nights—first in the ER and then on her honeymoon.

She felt another pang remembering the tenderness in Gabe's touch. Cursing her weakness, she went back to the bathroom to splash cold water on her face and cool the burn of tears behind her eyes.

Heading out into the kitchen, she found Nana, her nurse and Nadine dancing around. Nana, with one arm in a cast and sling, wore a baby carrier strapped to her front, with a fascinated Jason tucked inside. The child stared up at her as if she was the most fascinating person on earth, which Brianne could appreciate, even as she hoped her grandmother was truly strong enough to bear the extra weight of the baby.

"Woo-hoo, Brianne!" Nana called to her. "Look at me! I have a little one to love on. Isn't he the sweetest?"

Nadine stopped dancing, looking worried. "We tried to talk her out of it, Miss Brianne, I swear we tried."

"I've been keeping track of her vitals," Adella said quickly. "She's been doing so well."

"I've got a nurse on one side and a nanny on the other," Rose said, slowing down her moves as the music came to a stop. "I told them I've never been safer. And besides, this baby, he loves to dance." She rubbed noses with Jason, making him laugh.

Brianne's heart melted. She'd missed Jason so much. Her first thought was that she wished Gabe was here to see all the love lavished on his child. And damn if her eyes didn't start burning all over again. She wanted to be a family with him. With Jason.

"Honey, what's wrong?" Rose must have noticed Brianne's expression, because her own clouded over. "You're not worried about me, I hope."

"Here, Rose, let's get you back in a chair," Adella urged her. "I can show your granddaughter those vitals of yours that are better than most people half your age."

Working as a team, Nadine lifted Jason from the baby carrier while Adella unfastened the straps, freeing Rose from the cloth contraption. In the kitchen, Brianne belatedly noticed the homey Valentine's Day preparations. The romantic holiday was just a few days away. Heart-shaped sugar cookies cooled on a wire rack on the sleek gray granite countertop, and the whole kitchen was scented with vanilla and a hint of almond. A glass bowl of pink icing sat nearby, along with a half-dozen jars of candy decorations.

Nearby, at the table in the breakfast nook, there were paper hearts in a long chain, with multiple sets of scissors littered around the table. No doubt the group of women had been working on the heart chain when they got inspired to dance. A few toys were scattered on the spotless kitchen floor along with a plastic bowl and wooden spoon.

Rose had a seat at the breakfast nook while Nadine took the baby to the fridge to look over his lunch options. Adella retrieved a blood-pressure cuff and wrapped it around Rose's good arm.

"Honey, come sit with me." Rose gestured to the seat on the opposite side of the table. "Enjoy this beautiful day in the most beautiful apartment I've ever seen." Rose tipped her head toward the weak winter sun streaming in through the windows, where Central Park was visible. "Tell me about your honeymoon and how married life is treating you."

And that's all it took.

Brianne was mortified as she burst into tears.

An hour later, she'd shared the whole tale.

From her ill-fated crush on her boss-turned-best-friend, to the day she got Nana's letter and Gabe's suggestion they marry, to the basic details of the marriage contract.

"You shouldn't have run out during that dinner," Nana said finally, cutting out a few more paper hearts from the stack of pink, red and white construction paper. Despite her cast, she used both hands well enough. Apparently Adella had brought the paper with her to make decorations and valentines for the retirement home where she worked on the weekends.

Brianne was decorating the cookies, taking comfort from lavishing frosting and pretty candies on the sweets so that *someone*—namely, Adella's patients—would enjoy their Valentine's Day. She hated to think of how poor Jason would be spending the day: getting hauled to a photo studio for a promotional shoot with a woman he barely knew.

"I didn't run out," Brianne argued, digging in her heels on that point. "I wanted to give Gabe the time and space to work things out with his ex-wife."

Rose made a skeptical sound. "Sure sounds like you ran out to me. And his whole family was so nice to you."

"They were nice." From Brock giving her a ride, to Maisie and Malcolm insisting on sitting beside her, and Scarlett doing her best to divert Gabe's ex. "But don't you think Gabe needs to work things out with Theresa so they have a reasonable coparenting relationship?" Brianne asked. But a part of her so desperately wanted someone to give her a rock-solid reason why she was wrong to be afraid.

"She gave up her child—that beautiful, beautiful boy—before she ever laid eyes on him. Doesn't matter that she spent a couple of weeks with him after he was born. She told your Gabe that she wasn't ready to be a mother long before that, and that's okay. Not every woman dreams of having a baby to complete her and make her happy." Nana set down her scissors. "Maybe she's a better person for acknowledging that up front than someone like your own mama or stepmama, who were—excuse my saying so—sorry excuses for parents."

"Maybe so," Brianne admitted. "But it's Gabe who needs to work things out with her. Not me."

"There's bound to be a lot of hurt in that relationship, Brianne. You agreed to be his wife for at least a year. I would say that means you'll fight in his corner, or at the very least, be by his side during the awkward dinner parties." She met Brianne's gaze over her pink paper. "Marriage hasn't changed that much since back in my day."

Worry niggled at Brianne. "You think I chickened out?"

"I think you love this man like a house afire." Rose pointed at Brianne with the safety scissors. "And you're running away from the chance to make a real marriage with him. Call it what you will."

Ouch. Regret stung her hard.

"I was trying to do the right thing, Nana." Had she screwed up? Should she have stayed in Cheyenne and tried to work things out with Gabe? "I just can't bear the thought of him settling for me, you know? Like second prize at the fair."

She'd been selfish. Just like his horrible ex.

Nana put down her paper and scissors and shoved them aside. "Brianne, that man is a McNeill. Women in this city would form a nice neat line around the block for a chance to date him, let alone marry him. He chose *you* because he already trusted you and he liked you. You've been his closest friend. And now, he thinks he loves you? Call me crazy, but I don't know why you wouldn't believe him."

Because she was scared. It had taken her a lifetime to work up the courage to have sex after her first time was such a disappointing embarrassment. Maybe she needed to start taking more chances. To risk embarrassment or getting her heart broken.

"You're right." She finished decorating the last of the cookies and set the knife on top of the frosting bowl. "I need to call him. Or go back there. Or… what do you think I should do?"

Rose pursed her lips. "I've actually got some inside information about this."

"What do you mean?" Brianne heard Nadine singing a song to Jason a few rooms away.

"I've been texting with Malcolm."

Stunned, Brianne could only stare at her grandmother. "Malcolm? As in Malcolm McNeill?"

"He sent out a tweet about the wedding, you know." She retrieved her phone. "I have you to thank for my fancy new unlimited data plan. Because I've had a blast texting with him. Do you know he saw me perform at the Stork Club? I can't believe he re-members, that was so long ago." Nana patted her hair and laughed.

Suddenly, the dancing and the party in the kitchen made all the more sense. Nana had been raving about the lovely day, and she was as happy as Brianne could ever recall seeing her.

"Nana. You've been flirting with my grandfather-in-law."

"Maybe I have." Rose shrugged a shoulder. "At my age, I've learned to wrap my arms around the happy moments and hold tight. Tomorrow, I could be back on Bushwick Avenue. But today, look at me in a Central Park hotel apartment like I'm queen of Manhattan."

"Good for you, Nana. He seems like a nice man. And he's very handsome." Brianne could picture that nice, gentlemanly Malcolm McNeill flirting with her grandmother. And how adorable was it that they had a social-media relationship? "But you said you had inside information about what was happening be-tween Gabe and me. What did you mean? Did Gabe's grandfather share anything about what's happening in Cheyenne?"

She couldn't help the hopefulness in her voice. She ached for a chance to make things right with Gabe, if he would still listen to her after the way she'd walked out on him.

"He did." Nana leaned across the table. "He told me—"

A commotion erupted from the living room. A

door opened and closed, and exclamations went up all around—Jason, Nadine and a deeper, masculine voice that was so familiar it hurt.

Brianne felt hope and fear tangle in a fierce knot inside her belly.

Nana straightened in her seat. "Well, the cat's out of the bag now. Sounds like your husband is home, Brianne."

Fourteen

Brianne's old crush on her boss might have died a swift and brutal death when he'd walked down the aisle with another woman. But as she faced Gabe McNeill again in the living room of the luxuriously appointed apartment—no doubt with eavesdroppers posted at every doorway—she knew that the death of the crush had only made her real feelings for him deepen.

He would always be staggeringly handsome, charming and wealthier than any man had a right to be. Yet none of those reasons accounted for why she loved him. She just hoped she could make him understand how she felt and why she'd walked away despite his love for her.

Because Nana was right. She'd been too scared to take a risk. But not anymore.

Now, with Nadine whisking away Jason to give them at least the illusion of privacy, Brianne and Gabe were alone in the living room. She took in the dark suit he had worn for the flight and the aviator sunglasses propped in his hair. As he set a leather duffel bag on the floor at his feet, she studied him more closely, noticing the weary lines around his eyes from traveling. Or was some of that exhaustion more of an emotional variety, like hers? The need to wrap him in her arms was so strong she had to shove her hands in the pockets of her olive-colored cargo pants. She searched for the right words.

"Gabe—"

"Brianne—"

They began at the exact same time, but were out of synch with one another in every way possible.

"A gentleman would let you speak first," Gabe continued after a pause, plucking the sunglasses off his head and setting them on a sofa table. "But I've thought so damn hard about what I would say to you if you gave me the chance." He shook his head. "I don't want to lose my place."

Surprised that a man like Gabe would ever be at a loss for words, she simply nodded. But even as she agreed to listen first, she half feared she'd made a mistake. What if he pulled the plug on them before she had a chance to take her risk with him?

He waved her toward a pair of high-backed chairs positioned side by side looking out onto Central Park. She took a seat blindly, worry twisting her stomach.

Gabe lowered himself to the seat next to her. "Brianne, I know you saw what it was like for me when Theresa left," he began.

The ache in her gut only deepened as she nodded.

"I fought for her to stay, but not because I was so madly in love with her. I know that makes me a bad husband, but I was furious with myself for falling for a woman so fickle that she rejected our child like that." The haunted look that passed through Gabe's eyes might always be there, she realized.

Maybe this was something that would always be a part of him. Something he'd never "get over."

Empathy had her reaching for him. She laid her hand on his forearm and squeezed. "I know that was awful for you."

"It's awful for Jason," he responded, correcting her, his gaze holding a sense of purpose and an absolute clarity about the situation. "My feelings for her died, but I would have been right there beside her forever, doing everything I could to be a good family man if she had shown any interest in raising Jason together."

"I know that." Brianne nodded, picking through all the things she'd come to understand and love about Gabe. "It's one of the reasons that I was scared to believe you when you said you loved me. I know you have that tenacity to protect your child at all costs, and to do anything to make his life better."

Gabe shook his head. "Brianne, I fought for you— and I'm going to keep fighting for you—because I love *you*. I love who you are, and that doesn't have anything to do with Jason."

Surprise had her wishing she could rewind his words and listen to them again. Had he really just said that he wanted to keep fighting for her?

"But you married me for Jason's sake," she said, even though that wasn't at all what she meant to say. She needed to tell him she'd love him forever.

"Because I knew I could trust him with you. You'd never hurt him—and I don't think you'd hurt me, either, if you could help it." He took her hand that she had let linger on his arm and flipped it over. Tracing soft touches along her palm, he stared into her eyes. "That's one of many things that I love about you. You're so good with Jason. So warmhearted and easy to be around. I was falling for you long before I should have. But I didn't marry you for Jason's sake, no matter what I spouted at that time."

"You didn't?" Her words were barely there, just a hint of sound, as fragile as the hope that curled all around them.

"Absolutely not. It was easier to tell myself that I wanted you in my life for practical purposes because then I didn't have to face how much I already cared about you."

Brianne thought she heard a feminine whisper from behind the open archway that led into the kitchen, but it might have just been the voice in her head that sounded a lot like Nana, urging her to speak up.

"I was scared to let myself love you." She announced it without finesse or segue, awkward to the bitter end around this man she loved so very much. "I knew you'd lost so much faith in love and marriage—and who could blame you—so I worried you'd always carry some of that bitterness with you. That you wouldn't allow yourself to ever truly love again."

The blue of Gabe's eyes shifted somehow as he looked at her. There was something different in his expression that was special. Just for her. She could feel it, and it wrapped around her heart and squeezed tight.

"Don't be scared." He stroked a knuckle along her cheek like she was the most precious thing on earth. "I'd do anything to protect you, Brianne. I'd never, ever hurt you."

A watery smile trembled on her lips. "I love you, Gabriel McNeill. And if you'll have me back in your life as your wife, I promise I'll never run out on you again."

He captured her mouth for a kiss, inhaling the last of her words and soothing all that fractious, fearful hope, turning it into simple, delicious pleasure. When he broke the kiss, he gazed into her eyes like he had all the time in the world for her.

"And I promise you there won't be any more awkward dinner parties with my ex."

"There will be, though. She's going to waltz into Jason's first violin recital and his kindergarten graduation and expect us all to be very impressed with her." Brianne would find a way to deal with her, to keep the peace while promoting healthy boundaries. "But that's okay. She was right about one thing. She'll always be family. Together, we'll figure out times that she can be a part of Jason's life in a happy way."

"You're amazing," Gabe told her with a soft reverence that made her heart do a little tap dance. "And I might not deserve you, but I'm so glad you're going to give me a chance to be the best husband you could have ever imagined."

"You already are." She flung her arms around his neck, needing to hold him tight so she could feel the reality of him. Of this magical, delectable love. "You gave me Nana."

This time, there was no denying the feminine chortle of satisfaction Brianne heard from the eavesdropper on the other side of the wall. But it didn't matter. It would save her from having to recount the whole story.

Gabe's eyes darted toward the archway as he grinned. "Is it just me, or are we not alone in celebrating this love?"

From behind the archway there was a scuffle before Nana entered the room, holding up her phone and pointing the lens of the camera toward them. "Well, shoot, if my cover is blown, I'd like to at least have a nice photo to send to your granddaddy, young man. He's as invested as I am in finding out how the story turns out."

Brianne leaned in to Gabe and smiled for the picture while Nana's camera flashed. Adella took a tentative step into the room behind her. She was followed by Nadine holding Jason, who had probably only been quiet for this long because he was eating a Valentine cookie. Red frosting decorated both his cheeks. His dark curls bounced as he bopped to the tune he seemed to hear in his head.

"Gah!" he announced between bites.

Brianne's heart was so full she feared she would burst into tears for the second time that morning. Instead, she swallowed back that swell of emotion and cupped Gabe's face with her hands, knowing that all her dreams would come true with this man at her side.

"I love you so much, Gabe." She kissed his lips, but it was a teeth-knocking kiss since they were both grinning. "We're going to have the best time being married and loving each other for the rest of our lives."

"I'm never going to let you forget that you're the only woman to have my heart, Brianne." His words felt so right, honest and true. "Forever."

Epilogue

Seven months later

"**Y**ou must feel like you won the lottery living here every day," Scarlett McNeill observed between sips of a fruity umbrella drink. She jabbed at a lemon wedge with her straw, jiggling ice as she lay on a beach lounger beside Brianne.

Gabe's youngest cousin had come for a vacation to escape the ranch life in Cheyenne. But her official pretext for the visit had been to help Brianne get the nursery ready for the daughter she was expecting three months from now.

Already, her pregnant belly made a mound she had to stare over when she looked out at the crystalline blue water of the Caribbean Sea. Not that she minded. She still wore a bikini to admire the miracle of a life growing inside her.

So what if she hadn't made much headway on the nursery since Scarlett's arrival? Gabe's cousin made an excellent sunbathing companion. For the first time in Brianne's life, she was taking a real, honest-to-goodness vacation, having abandoned all her landscape-design chores at the Birdsong. Gabe had been hiding her pruning shears on a regular basis anyhow, insisting she rest and focus on baby-brewing.

And with Scarlett around, she had a partner in crime to accompany her to the beach every day. When they weren't reading juicy romance novels or trading opinions on the growing relationship between Rose and Malcolm McNeill, they spent time playing in the kitchen, blending tasty fruity drinks—without alcohol for Brianne and with alcohol for Scarlett.

"That's exactly how I feel," Brianne observed, stirring her mango-passion fruit concoction while she flipped through a magazine full of nursery décor ideas. "Every day is like a lottery win with Gabe."

She had moved into his cottage on the property while he added on a huge addition to accommodate their growing family. She didn't want anything too big, and she hadn't wanted to build off-site since she had so many happy memories right here on the Birdsong property. They'd fallen in love while she gardened and he built things, so as far as Brianne was concerned, they could spend every day that same way for the rest of their lives.

Gabe had indulged her, but he was sparing no expense on the addition to the Key West-style "bungalow" with enough square footage to house most of the McNeills whenever they wanted to visit.

"'With Gabe.'" Scarlett mimicked Brianne and rolled her eyes, swiping her dark curls into a high ponytail with a pink elastic band she'd been using for a bracelet. "You're such a newlywed. I'm sure life with my cute cousin is wonderful, but when I mentioned the lottery win, I was thinking more along the lines of this view. This weather. The exotic flowers everywhere. It's paradise."

Listening to the waves roll onto the shore with their calming music, she had to agree.

"It is just about perfect. But I'm bringing the kids to Cheyenne next winter so we can play in the snow." And at the rate Malcolm was going, flying Rose to New York and Cheyenne for frequent visits, Brianne would need to go there to see her grandmother anyhow.

At least Nana had promised to be in Martinique for the birth of the baby.

"Snow. Ugh." Scarlett tipped her face into the breeze. "Maybe I'll house-sit for you when you're up there."

"House-sit?" A shadow fell over Brianne as her husband entered the conversation. "I'm wondering if you'll consider babysitting, since I'd like to steal my beautiful wife for a few minutes."

Brianne's whole world lit up as she glimpsed Gabe trying to hold Jason's hand before the little sprite sprinted into the surf. At almost a year and a half, the boy ran everywhere, his legs churning nonstop all day long until he fell into an exhausted sleep at eight o'clock every night.

"Mama!" Jason patted Brianne's belly gently, slowing down long enough to very careful with her.

A McNeill already.

Scarlett came to her feet. "You mean I get to play with this cutie?" She scooped Jason up for a kiss before putting him back down so he could run toward the shoreline. "I like that trade."

The two of them squealed and splashed on the beach, dancing along the waves.

"I quite like that trade, too." Gabe kissed Brianne's forehead and then her cheek. Then her lips. And that kiss lingered. "How are my girls today? Do you want to go for a walk with me?"

She squinted up at him in the sunlight, loving the way a light sheen of sawdust still covered his upper arms. He must have been working on the addition.

"I'll go most anywhere with you, Gabe." She started to get up, but before she was off her chair, he was tucking an arm under her elbow and guiding her to her feet. "And both of your girls are happy as can be."

"Good." His smile was possessive and all-male as his gaze raked over her. "Have I mentioned how much I love the bathing suit?"

"You might have worked that into conversation

a few times." She grinned at him, giving his side a light pinch. "Especially since all I've done is laze around on the beach since Scarlett arrived."

"I couldn't have come up with a better way to distract you myself. I'm a whole lot happier seeing you in a bikini than battling vines and roots with the gardening shears."

Brianne tipped her forehead against his shoulder, inhaling the light scent of sweat and sawdust that was a serious turn-on.

"Doesn't it feel like every day we've won the lottery?" she asked, thinking Scarlett had really nailed it with that observation.

Gabe slowed his step and stopped, turning to look in her eyes. "Every. Single. Day."

* * * * *

#2575 MARRIED FOR HIS HEIR
Billionaires and Babies • by Sara Orwig
Reclusive rancher Nick is shocked to learn he's a father to an orphaned baby girl! Teacher Talia loves the baby as her own. So Nick proposes they marry for the baby—with no hearts involved. But he's about to learn a lesson about love...

#2576 A CONVENIENT TEXAS WEDDING
Texas Cattleman's Club: The Impostor
by Sheri WhiteFeather
A Texas millionaire must change his playboy image or lose everything he's worked for. An innocent Irish miss needs a green card immediately after her ex's betrayal. The rule for their marriage of convenience: don't fall in love. For these two opposites, rules are made to be broken...

#2577 THE DOUBLE DEAL
Alaskan Oil Barons • by Catherine Mann
Wild child Naomi Steele chose to get pregnant with twins, and she'll do anything to earn a stake for them in her family's oil business. Even if that means confronting an isolated scientist in a blizzard. But the man is sexier than sin and the snowstorm is moving in... Dare she mix business with pleasure?

#2578 LONE STAR LOVERS
Dallas Billionaires Club • by Jessica Lemmon
PR consultant Penelope Brand vowed to never, ever get involved with a client again. But then her latest client turns out to be her irresistible one-night stand, and he introduces her as his fiancée. Now she's playing couple, giving in to temptation...and expecting the billionaire's baby.

#2579 TAMING THE BILLIONAIRE BEAST
Savannah Sisters • by Dani Wade
When she arrives on a remote Southern island to become temporary housekeeper at a legendary mansion, Willow Harden finds a beastly billionaire boss in reclusive Tate Kingston. But he's also the most tempting man she's ever met. Will she fall prey to his seduction...or to the curse of Sabatini House?

#2580 SAVANNAH'S SECRETS
The Bourbon Brothers • by Reese Ryan
Savannah Carlisle infiltrated a Tennessee bourbon empire for revenge, *not* to fall for the seductive heir of it all. But as the potential for scandal builds and one *little* secret exposes everything, will it cost her the love of a man she was raised to hate?

PR consultant Penelope Brand vowed to never, ever get involved with a client again. But then her latest client turns out to also be her irresistible one-night stand, and he introduces her as his fiancée.

Now she's playing couple, giving in to temptation…and might soon be expecting the billionaire's baby…

Read on for a sneak peek at
LONE STAR LOVERS
by Jessica Lemmon, the first book in the
***DALLAS BILLIONAIRES CLUB** trilogy!*

"You'll get to meet my brother tonight."

Penelope was embarrassed she didn't know a thing about another Ferguson sibling. She'd only been in Texas for a year, and between juggling her new business, moving into her apartment and handling crises for the Dallas elite, she hadn't climbed the Ferguson family tree any higher than Chase and Stefanie.

"Perfect timing," Chase said, his eyes going over her shoulder to welcome a new arrival.

"Hey, hey, big brother."

Now, that…that was a drawl.

The back of her neck prickled. She recognized the voice instantly. It sent warmth pooling in her belly and lower. It stood her nipples on end. The Texas accent over her shoulder was a tad thicker than Chase's, but not as lazy as it'd been two weeks ago. Not like it was when she'd invited him home and he'd leaned close, his lips brushing the shell of her ear.

Lead the way, gorgeous.

Squaring her shoulders, Pen prayed Zach had the shortest memory ever, and turned to make his acquaintance.

Correction: reacquaintance.

She was floored by broad shoulders outlined by a sharp black tux, longish dark blond hair smoothed away from his handsome face and the greenest eyes she'd ever seen. Zach had been gorgeous the first time she'd laid eyes on him, but his current look suited the air of control and power swirling around him.

A primal, hidden part of her wanted to lean into his solid form and rest in his capable, strong arms again. As tempting as reaching out to him was, she wouldn't. She'd had her night with him. She was in the process of assembling a firm bedrock for her fragile, rebuilt business and she refused to let her world fall apart because of a sexy man with a dimple.

A dimple that was notably missing since he was gaping at her with shock. His poker face needed work.

"I'll be damned," Zach muttered. "I didn't expect to see you here."

"That makes two of us," Pen said, and then she polished off half her champagne in one long drink.

Don't miss
LONE STAR LOVERS
by Jessica Lemmon, the first book in the
DALLAS BILLIONAIRES CLUB *trilogy!*

Available March 2018 wherever
Harlequin® Desire books and ebooks are sold.

www.Harlequin.com

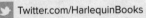
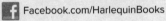
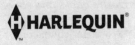

LOVE
Harlequin
romance?

Join our Harlequin community to share your thoughts and connect with other romance readers!

Be the first to find out about promotions, news, and exclusive content!

Sign up for the Harlequin e-newsletter and download a free book from any series at

www.TryHarlequin.com

CONNECT WITH US AT:

Harlequin.com/Community

 Facebook.com/HarlequinBooks

 Twitter.com/HarlequinBooks

 Instagram.com/HarlequinBooks

 Pinterest.com/HarlequinBooks

ReaderService.com

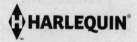 **HARLEQUIN**®

**ROMANCE WHEN
YOU NEED IT**

HSOCIAL2017

Earn points from all your Harlequin book purchases from wherever you shop.

Turn your points into *FREE BOOKS* of your choice
OR
EXCLUSIVE GIFTS from your favorite authors or series.

Join for FREE today at
www.HarlequinMyRewards.com.

Harlequin My Rewards is a free program (no fees) without any commitments or obligations.

MYR17